The World Almanac of Football

The Kids' World Almanac of Football

by BILL GUTMAN

WORLD ALMANAC BOOKS

An Imprint of Funk & Wagnalls Corporation

Library of Congress Catalog Card Number: 94-71338

ISBN: 0-88687-765-2 (hardcover)
ISBN: 0-88687-764-4 (softcover)

Printed in the United States of America.

Design by Bill Smith Studio
Illustrations by Bernard Adnet
Cover design by Nathaniel Estes

World Almanac® Books
An Imprint of Funk & Wagnalls Corporation
One International Boulevard
Mahwah, NJ 07495-0017

10 9 8 7 6 5 4 3 2 1

DEDICATION

For Cathy

About the Author

Bill Gutman is the author of more than 120 books for children and adults. He began his writing career as a reporter on a daily newspaper in Greenwich, Connecticut, and later became the paper's sports editor.

His first book was a biography of former basketball great Pistol Pete Maravich, which was chosen as a *Sports Illustrated* Sports-Book-of-the-Month Club alternate selection. Since that time, Mr. Gutman has written biographies of many top sports stars, including Hank Aaron, Julius Erving, Pele, Bo Jackson, Michael Jordan, David Robinson, Magic Johnson, and Shaquille O'Neal.

He has also written a series of sports instructional books for children (*Go for It*), as well as several sports novels, three of which were highly recommended by the American Library Association.

His nonsports books include biographies of jazz great Duke Ellington and former President Andrew Jackson. In addition, he has written histories of pro and college basketball, as well as a history of major league baseball between 1941 and 1964.

Bill Gutman was born in New York City and grew up in Stamford, Connecticut. He received a B.A. from Washington College in Chestertown, Maryland, and did graduate work at the University of Bridgeport in Connecticut. Mr. Gutman presently lives in Poughquag, New York, with his wife, Cathy, stepson, Allen, and a variety of pets.

CONTENTS

The Kids' World Almanac of Football

INTRODUCTION

Football, football, and more football. This is what both the casual and the rabid fan will find crammed between the covers of THE KIDS' WORLD ALMANAC OF FOOTBALL. The great players, championship games, and record performances, those strange and amazing gridiron moments, as well as tons of interesting trivia … it's all here.

This is a book that was both fun and fascinating to research. It meant going back to the beginnings of the game, learning how the sport of football originated and evolved, and also relating tales of the gridiron's early heroes, who played at a time when the game was very different from football today.

You'll read about the very first professional football player, a man with the unlikely name of "Pudge" Heffelfinger. And you'll learn about George Gipp, the legendary Notre Dame halfback known as the Gipper. There is also the story of Jim Thorpe, one of the greatest football players ever, who once started a professional team called the Oorang Indians.

Since the ALMANAC includes the worlds of both college and professional football, there is twice as much excitement. On the pro side there's everything from information on all the National Football League teams to profiles of the top players from both the past and the present to recaps of all the championship games and Super Bowls.

There are dramatizations of the great records, set by everyone from "Slingin'" Sammy Baugh to O.J. Simpson to Dan Marino. You will also find the strange and unusual happenings that have occurred on the gridiron and all kinds of fun trivia with which to surprise and astound your friends. There is a section on Canadian Football, a pro game with some slightly different twists from the American version.

The college sections also contain a wealth of record-breaking performances, wild and wacky happenings, and more trivia. How many football fans know, for instance, that chariot races were once held at the Rose Bowl instead of a New Year's Day football game? Read the ALMANAC and find out why.

There are all kinds of lists—draft choices, Heisman Trophy winners, national champions, all-time team and coaching records. Add to all this quotes from many of the game's greats, a complete glossary of gridiron terms, and descriptions of the skills needed to play each position, and you have a package chock-full of football.

The goal with THE KIDS' WORLD ALMANAC OF FOOTBALL was to produce the most complete book of its kind, and I feel we have succeeded. You can open to any page and find something new and exciting. Reference book, fun book, trivia book, stat book, a book loaded with anecdotes. It all spells ALMANAC. And it was great fun putting it all together.

Bill Gutman
August 1994

The Early Days

1920 STALEY TEAM

Like most sports, football didn't just "happen" overnight. It wasn't a case of someone saying, "Let's play football," and the next day there was a 100-yard-long field, neatly lined and ready to go, 11 players on each side, a leather-covered football, officials, and a stadium full of fans. The game evolved out of a series of events taking place over hundreds of years. Part of football comes from soccer, part from rugby, and part from plain ol' organized mayhem.

People have played various kinds of kicking games since the earliest of times. The ancient Greeks called their kicking game harpaston. In Italy during the Middle Ages the game was called calcia. In England during the 12th century there was a wild game that came to be known as futballe.

The "ball" in these early games could be almost anything. Rocks were used. So was shredded bamboo and moss stuffed into a leather hide. Later a cow's or pig's bladder was inflated and sometimes covered by a leather hide.

One of the strangest of the early footballs was used in 11th-century England. There was a Danish invasion of England in 1016 and the Danes occupied the country until 1042, when they were driven out. Some years later, old battlefields were plowed for farmland. Whenever a Danish skull surfaced, the English began a game of futballe, kicking the skull around the field.

TOWN AND COLLEGE PRIDE AT STAKE

In the early days there were no 100,000-seat stadiums packed to the rafters with fans rooting for their team. But there were crowds. In 12th-century England, large numbers of people gathered in the streets to watch groups of men and boys play a football game without boundary lines. Any landmark might be a goal. In the course of a game, fences were knocked down, gardens trampled, and people hurt.

Often one village played against another. There was so much pride at stake that the games sometimes resulted in a free-for-all between the competing communities. In the eyes of some, football during the Middle Ages was more of an unorganized shoving match than a sport.

When the game came to colonial America, the same unruliness prevailed. It was played in the streets, with wild swarms of youths running helter-skelter. Later, the game took on the same form at colleges and universities. It became an annual contest between sophomores and freshmen.

Known as the "rush," the game began when a bold freshman had the nerve to touch the rubber or leather ball that was used. What happened next was akin to a big brawl. Both teams threw themselves forward, with hands, feet, elbows, and fists flying. The game ended when the ball somehow worked its way through the ranks of one of the classes and emerged behind them. The other class was then declared the winner.

BLOODY MONDAY

Harvard University, founded in 1636, has long been known as one of the great centers of education in the United States. But years ago Harvard freshmen and sophomores met in an annual rush that was so brutal it became known as Bloody Monday. There were so many lost teeth and broken bones that Harvard abolished the rush in 1860. It was reintroduced about 20 years later, but by that time it resembled soccer. The hands couldn't be used, and the players didn't get hurt nearly as much.

Football as we know it today wasn't far off.

THE FIRST RUNNER
AND OTHER DEVELOPMENTS

In Rugby, England, back in 1823, a schoolboy named William Webb Ellis decided he was bored just kicking the ball. In the middle of a game he suddenly picked the ball up and began running with it. Though this was against the rules, the action of running through people with the ball excited both the crowd and the players. Ellis's action led to the development of rugby, one of the forerunners of modern football. At Eton in England, the field that the players used was big enough for only about 11 players on each side, and over time the American football game settled on this number of participants.

By the 1840s football, even if it was just the freshman-sophomore rush, was being played at all Ivy League colleges in the United States. It was, to say the least, a very rough game. At Yale students developed the flying wedge, a tactic in which blockers locked arms, formed a "V" around the ballcarrier, and ran at full speed. It was a vicious blocking formation that led to many injuries and would eventually be outlawed from football.

THE FIRST GAME

Although the contest between Princeton and Rutgers on November 6, 1869, has long been known as the first real football game in America, the two teams were basically playing soccer. A game closer to football was played between Harvard and Yale on November 13, 1875, at New Haven, Connecticut. The teams used a variation of rugby rules and attracted a crowd of more than 2,000 fans.

A year later, in 1876, Yale, Harvard, Princeton, and Columbia formed the Intercollegiate Football Association. They played a game that used both rugby and soccer rules. That same year, a Yale freshman joined his school's football team. He loved the game but soon saw that it wasn't complete. His name was Walter Camp, and over the next two decades he would change the face of the new sport.

THE FATHER OF
AMERICAN FOOTBALL

After playing seven years for Yale, Walter Camp became the "Eli" coach. His assistant was his wife, Allie. The game Camp played at Yale had two 45-minute halves. Substitutions were allowed only for injury. There was no line of scrimmage. Instead, play began with the players locking shoulders as in a rugby scrum.

Players argued with umpires constantly. The rowdiness during games led an Englishman, Stephen Leacock, to proclaim: "The Americans are a queer people. They can't play football. They try to, but they can't. They turn football into a fight."

Walter Camp

That was before Walter Camp led the campaign to change things. In 1880, largely as a result of Camp's efforts, the number of players on each side was reduced to 11. Camp also was the prime mover in developing play from the line of scrimmage. This innovation, in which the center snapped the ball into the backfield to start a play, allowed the offensive team to plan plays in advance.

The scene was now set for the introduction of the quarterback, who would eventually call signals for the entire offensive unit. Camp also encouraged the rules committee to adopt a regulation in 1882 giving a team three chances (known as "downs") to gain five yards. When opponents of this rule change complained that there was no way to accurately measure gains and losses, Camp came up with the idea of marking the field with chalk lines every five yards. It was the start of the modern "gridiron."

The point system was also modified in the 1880s under Camp's direction. First one point was awarded for a safety, two for a touchdown, and five for a field goal. By 1884 a touchdown was worth four points, and a conversion and a safety were worth two points each.

In the 1890s the sport was becoming more popular, and it was looking more like football as we know it today. The ball was still big, but it was becoming more oblong than round.

THE MODERN RULES TAKE SHAPE

As the years passed the game continued to change. In 1888 tackling below the waist was legalized. In rugby, it was against the rules. Because the ball-carrier's legs were now a target, more padding—especially protection for the knees and shins—became part of the standard football uniform. Headgear was also added, beginning with small, knit caps that were worn mostly by fullbacks. In 1897, Glenn S. "Pop" Warner, coach of the Carlisle Indians, fitted his team with headgear and in time it became a regular part of the uniform. The value of a touchdown went from four points to five in 1898, and to its present-day six points in 1912. A field goal was changed from five points to four in 1904. Then, in 1909, it was dropped to the present-day three.

Although college teams had been throwing the football for years, the forward pass was not legalized in the pro game until 1906.

Blocking rules were changing as well. Players could no longer use hands and extended arms. Teams at the Carlisle Indian School also began using a rolling block to take an opponent's legs out from under him.

PUDGE TAKES PAY FOR PLAY

As the sport of football grew during the latter part of the 19th century, it seemed only a matter of time before someone decided to start a professional team. The first football player to admit he was being paid to play was William W. "Pudge" Heffelfinger, who played guard at Yale from 1889 to 1891. Heffelfinger was a member of the first Walter Camp All-American team in 1889. He made the team for three straight years.

A year after graduating from Yale in 1891, Heffelfinger was paid $500 to play a game with the Allegheny Athletic Association of Pittsburgh. Allegheny was playing its arch rival, the Pittsburgh Athletic Club, and wanted Heffelfinger's help.

The game was played on November 12, 1892, and Allegheny's investment paid off. The only score came when Heffelfinger picked up an Athletic Club fumble and ran 35 yards for a touchdown. Allegheny won the game, 4-0 (a TD was worth four points then). Three years later the YMCA-sponsored team of Latrobe, Pennsylvania, hired quarterback John Brallier for $10 a game plus expenses. Latrobe's game against another Pennsylvania team, Jeanette, on August 31, 1895, is officially recognized as the first professional football game. (Latrobe won by a score of 12-0.)

THE PRO GAME IS HERE TO STAY

The Allegheny Athletic Association, the same team that paid Pudge Heffelfinger for his services, also fielded the first completely professional team in 1896. But the Athletic Association played only two games that year. A year later the Latrobe football team became the first club to play a full season using only professional players.

In 1902 a pair of professional baseball franchises also formed football teams. The Philadelphia Athletics and the Philadelphia Phillies joined the Pittsburgh Stars in attempting to form football's first professional league. They named it the National Football League.

The league was loosely organized that year, and all three teams claimed the championship. Then there was a five-team postseason tournament called the World Series of professional football. Syracuse (New York) was the eventual winner of the tournament, and finally league president David J. Berry proclaimed the Pittsburgh Stars the regular-season champion.

Pennsylvania was not the only center of football activity. By the early 1900's there were seven professional teams in the state of Ohio. Massillon defeated Akron for Ohio's first professional football championship in 1904. A year later Massillon defeated a new Ohio team, the Canton Bulldogs, for the state championship. Canton would later become the permanent home of the Pro Football Hall of Fame.

THE FORMATION OF THE NATIONAL FOOTBALL LEAGUE

Early professional football games were violent, hard to follow, and poorly organized. Several team sponsors, players, and coaches, realizing the need to bring pro football into a tighter organization, met in Akron, Ohio, in August 1920. This was followed by a more formal meeting a month later in Canton, at which time the American Professional Football Conference was formed. There were 14 teams that first year, but not all of them completed the schedule. The name of the league was then changed to the American Professional Football Association (APFA).

In 1921 there were 21 teams in the league, though teams like the Tonawanda (New York) Kardex, Muncie (Indiana) Flyers, and Louisville (Ohio) Brecks broke up after playing just one or two games. The Chicago Staleys were awarded the championship on the basis of a 9-1-1 record. The Staleys were purchased by player-coach George Halas and in 1922 became known as the Bears.

Also in 1922, the league changed its name. It was now the National Football League, and the National Football League it would remain. The best team was the Canton Bulldogs, finishing as champions with a 10-0-2 record.

College football grew at a much faster pace than the pro game. Colleges began to pack the fans in during the 1920s. Pro football took longer to become established, although it always had a strong core following. But one thing was for certain. After decades of development and change, football as an American sport was here to stay.

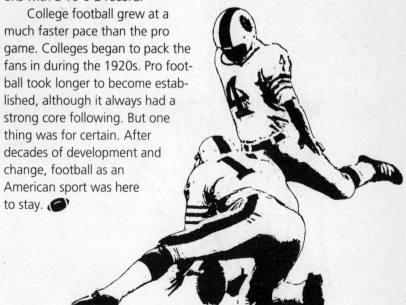

2

A Few
Names
From
the Past

Here are brief profiles of a few of the very earliest gridiron stars. Some may be forgotten names now, but each contributed to the growth of the sport in a very special way.

Pudge Heffelfinger

Not only was William W. "Pudge" Heffelfinger the first player to take pay for play, he was a man who loved the game of football and played it for several decades. In 1939, Heffelfinger gave an amazing interview to the famed sportswriter Grantland Rice.

"Who said football is a tough game?" said Heffelfinger. "I played it for 50 years. I know I was better at 45 than I was at 20. But I'll have to admit I slowed down a little when I was 66. Not much. But a little."

Pudge was telling the truth. At the age of 53 he played a full 60 minutes as part of an All-Star team opposing the Ohio State All-Stars. And when he was nearly 66 he suited up for a charity benefit game in Minneapolis, playing alongside men about one-third of his age. He died in 1954 at the age of 86.

Lawson Fiscus

Fiscus was a star player for Princeton in 1891-1892. A muscular halfback with a huge handlebar mustache, he was known as the Samson of Princeton. Fiscus was also the first player to take a regular paycheck for playing football. After leaving Princeton, Fiscus joined an independent pro team in Greensburg, Pennsylvania, and was paid $20 a week plus expenses for his services.

Though he had a gentlemanly appearance, Fiscus played the game in a blood-and-guts tradition. He once kicked a player from the Jeannette (Pennsylvania) team who was lying on the ground, breaking the man's jaw and stirring up so much anger that extra deputy sheriffs were always standing by when the two teams played after that.

The Nesser Family

Perhaps the Nesser family best represented the toughness and strength of the early pro football players. The Nessers were an immigrant family that came to America before the turn of the century. Soon they moved to Columbus, Ohio, where the men became boilermakers, working for the Pennsylvania Railroad.

None of the six Nessers who played football went to college, but that didn't stop them from falling in love with the game. By 1911 all six (five brothers and one brother's son) were in the starting lineup of the Columbus Panhandles. While the brothers played, their father served as a combination trainer and waterboy.

What all the Nessers had in common was toughness. John was a top quarterback, while Frank could punt the football from one end of the field to the other. Phil Nesser was such a fine all-around athlete that those who watched him play agreed he could have had scholarship offers from many colleges. Ted, Al, and Ted's son Fred were also exciting players.

Perhaps the toughest of them all was Al. He was a fearless defensive player who would take on the biggest and strongest of opponents without a second thought. He began playing football when he was a schoolboy in the 1890s and had a pro career that began in 1910 and lasted until 1931, when he was at end for the old Cleveland Indians. In all the years he played, Al never wore a helmet or pads of any kind. He never

Football family: The Nessers in a family photo.

even wore an athletic supporter. That's amazing when you consider how long he played and how rough the game was back then.

Willie Heston

Heston was a halfback at the University of Michigan and an All-American in both 1903 and 1904. A speedy, slashing runner, he was the star player on a Michigan team that won 43 games, tied one, and lost none during his time in Ann Arbor. In the 44 games in which Heston played, the Wolverines ran up 2,326 points while giving up fewer than 50. And during that time (1901-1904), Heston set an amazing record by scoring 100 touchdowns, a mark that still stands.

When his college career ended, Heston demanded $1,200 to play his first pro game. He finally settled for half that amount to play for Canton against Massillon in 1905. He failed to gain a single yard as Massillon won the game, 14-4. After that, Heston played only one other pro game (in Chicago), broke his leg, and retired.

George Gipp

Almost every football fan has heard the expression, "Win one

for the Gipper." But who was the real Gipper? He was a fun-loving, high-spirited, extremely talented halfback named George Gipp, who played for Notre Dame more than 70 years ago.

Gipp played under Notre Dame's legendary coach Knute Rockne and was a 175-pound broken-field runner. He could also drop-kick the ball some 65 yards. In one spectacular game, George Gipp ran for an amazing 332 yards. He left school in 1918 to serve in the army during World War I, then returned the next year greater than ever.

In 1920 Gipp had another All-American season. But coming into the final game against unbeaten Northwestern, he was on the bench with a bad cold. It was a bitter day and Coach Rockne didn't want to play him. But in the final quarter Gipp pleaded to go in, and when he did, he scored the winning touchdown with a typical broken-field run.

After the game, Gipp fell critically ill with a streptococcal infection and pneumonia. He died three weeks later, with Rockne at his side. The movie about Rockne's life, *Knute Rockne, All American* (1940), features a classic scene in which a dying George Gipp, played by Ronald Reagan, tells Rockne, "Some day when the going is tough, ask the boys to win one for the Gipper."

John Heisman

John Heisman was born in 1869, just four years after the end of the Civil War. He played college football at Brown University and the University of Pennsylvania, but was only an

The Heisman Trophy

average player. In 1892 Heisman took the head coaching job at Oberlin College, beginning a coaching career that would last 35 years.

Heisman also coached at Georgia Tech, Auburn, Clemson, Pennsylvania, Rice, and Washington & Jefferson. His teams won 185 games while losing just 70. That includes a Georgia Tech team that beat Cumberland College, 222-0, the most one-sided college victory ever.

A demanding, innovative coach, Heisman pioneered such things as a direct snap from center, the hidden-ball trick, and the backfield shift. His love of the game of football never waned, even after his retirement in 1927. He died in 1936 after falling from a tree which he had climbed to watch a sandlot football game.

Soon after Heisman died, a trophy that had been put up in 1935 to honor the best player in college football was named the Heisman Memorial Trophy. This award, first won by Jay Berwanger of Chicago, remains the most prized individual honor in college football.

Jim Thorpe

The most legendary name from football's early days, Jim Thorpe was a Sac-Fox Indian whom many still call the greatest athlete who ever lived. He played major league baseball and was a track and field Olympic champion and a professional football star. But it was as a collegian at the Carlisle Indian School in Pennsylvania that he achieved perhaps his greatest glory.

Thorpe was a 6'2", 185-pounder with a combination of blazing speed and incredible strength. He was rarely injured and played every minute of every game. Some say he was the hardest blocker they had ever seen, and his broken-field touchdown runs are legendary. He could also drop-kick 50-yard field goals and punt the football up to 80 yards.

Thorpe, as an All-American in 1911 and 1912, helped tiny Carlisle upset some of the best teams in the country. In 1912, he scored 25 touchdowns, kicked 38 field goals, and scored 198 points. When he joined the Canton Bulldogs in 1915 his great play helped put pro football on the map.

In the minds of many, this great player will always be *Jim Thorpe, All-American* (the title of a 1951 movie based on his life).

CHECK OUT THESE OLD TEAM NAMES

In the early days of the National Football League, franchises came and went. Some didn't even finish a single season. Many of these were small town teams, long forgotten except by diehard football fans. Here are some of the teams that played in the NFL between 1920 and 1930:

Decatur Staleys, Rock Island Independents, Hammond Pros, Columbus Panhandles, Muncie Flyers, Evansville Crimson Giants, Dayton Triangles, Rochester Jeffersons, Tonawanda Kardex, Louisville Brecks, Toledo Maroons, Racine Legion, Oorang Indians, Milwaukee Badgers, Duluth Kelleys, Cleveland Bulldogs.

Frankford Yellow Jackets, Kansas City Blues, Minneapolis Marines, Kenosha Maroons, Pottsville Maroons, Providence Steam Roller, Duluth Eskimos, Buffalo Rangers, Hartford Blues, Brooklyn Lions, Racine Tornadoes, New York Yankees, Orange Tornadoes, Staten Island Stapletons, Portsmouth Spartans, and Newark Tornadoes.

Try some of those on for size in today's NFL.

3
Today's
NFL Teams

In the 1990s the National Football League was bigger and better than ever. With the 1993 addition of two expansion teams, scheduled to begin play in 1995, there were 30 teams, 15 in the American Football Conference and 15 in the National Football Conference. Each conference is divided into Eastern, Central, and Western divisions. All teams are located in the continental United States, stretching from coast to coast.

Prior to the addition of the Carolina Panthers and the Jacksonville Jaguars in 1993, the last expansion had occurred in 1976, when Tampa Bay and Seattle joined the league. In the very early days, teams came and went with regularity. When divisional play began in 1933, there were just ten teams in the league. At one point, in 1943, only eight teams were in operation.

By 1960 the NFL was up to 13 teams, while the newly formed American Football League had eight. A decade later the two leagues merged into a bigger NFL with two conferences and 26 teams. The league has been extremely stable since that time.

HOW THE NFL IS SET UP

In 1994 the American Football Conference had five teams in the Eastern and Western divisions, and four in the Central. The National Football Conference was made up of five teams in the Eastern and Central divisions, four in the West.

Under the present setup, 12 teams make it to the playoffs, six from the NFC and six from the AFC. The divisional winners, of course, qualify automatically. In addition, "wild-card" spots are awarded to the three non-first-place finishers in each conference with the best won-lost records. In 1992 both Philadelphia and Washington from the NFC East made the playoffs as wild-card teams because both had better records than the second-place team in the Central Division.

The playoffs consist of four wild-card games, two each in the NFC and AFC. These are followed by four divisional playoff games (again, two in each conference), then two conference championship games (one per conference) and, finally, the Super Bowl, in which the NFC champion faces the AFC champion.

Bears' tight end Mike Ditka carries the ball against the Packers.

This is the way the teams were divided by conference and division in 1994.

NATIONAL FOOTBALL LEAGUE

AMERICAN FOOTBALL CONFERENCE	NATIONAL FOOTBALL CONFERENCE
Eastern Division Buffalo Bills Indianapolis Colts Miami Dolphins New England Patriots New York Jets	**Eastern Division** Arizona Cardinals Dallas Cowboys New York Giants Philadelphia Eagles Washington Redskins
Central Division Cincinnati Bengals Cleveland Browns Houston Oilers Pittsburgh Steelers	**Central Division** Chicago Bears Detroit Lions Green Bay Packers Minnesota Vikings Tampa Bay Buccaneers
Western Division Denver Broncos Kansas City Chiefs Los Angeles Raiders San Diego Chargers Seattle Seahawks	**Western Division** Atlanta Falcons Los Angeles Rams New Orleans Saints San Francisco 49ers

The following pages provide a quick look at each of the NFL teams, including some important facts and figures so you can get to know them better.

AMERICAN FOOTBALL CONFERENCE

Buffalo Bills

MAILING ADDRESS: One Bills Drive, Orchard Park, New York 14127. **TEAM COLORS:** Royal blue, scarlet red, and white. **PLAYING FIELD:** Rich Stadium (80,290). **SURFACE:** AstroTurf.

The Bills began play in 1960 as part of the old American Football League. The team joined the NFL with the merger in 1970. Buffalo was an early AFL power, winning a pair of league titles. In recent years, the Bills have become one of the best teams in the NFL. While they won four consecutive AFC championships from 1990 to 1993, they also had the misfortune of being the first team in NFL history to lose four straight Super Bowls.

Most remembered alumni: Quarterback (more recently secretary of housing and urban development in President George Bush's Cabinet) Jack Kemp; running back O. J. Simpson; kicker Pete Gogolak; wide receiver Elbert "Golden Wheels" Dubenion; guard Reggie McKenzie; quarterback Joe Ferguson.

Cincinnati Bengals

MAILING ADDRESS: 200 Riverfront Stadium, Cincinnati, Ohio 45202. **TEAM COLORS:** Black, orange, and white. **PLAYING FIELD:** Riverfront Stadium (60,389). **SURFACE:** AstroTurf-8.

The Bengals were an AFL expansion team in 1968 and coached by the legendary Paul Brown. Though the team has had an up-and-down existence, it won AFC titles in 1982 and 1989. However, the Bengals were beaten in both Super Bowl appearances, each time by the San Francisco 49ers.

Most remembered alumni: Quarterbacks Ken Anderson and Boomer Esiason; wide receivers Isaac Curtis and Cris Collinsworth; defensive end Ross Browner; running back James Brooks.

Cleveland Browns

MAILING ADDRESS: 80 First Avenue, Berea, Ohio 44017. **TEAM COLORS:** Seal brown, orange, and white. **PLAYING FIELD:** Cleveland Stadium (78,512). **SURFACE:** Grass.

The Browns have a storied history. The team started in the old All-America Football Conference in 1946 and were champions of the league in each of the four years it operated. Joining the NFL in 1950, the Browns shocked the football world by winning the NFL title. Between 1951 and 1965 Cleveland played in eight championship games, winning three times (1954, 1955, and 1964). The team won conference titles in 1968 and 1969. Since moving to the AFC after the 1970 merger, the Browns have lost three AFC title games. The team has never been to the Super Bowl.

Most remembered alumni: Coach Paul Brown; quarterbacks Otto Graham and Brian Sipe; tackle/placekicker Lou Groza; tackle Mike McCormack; running backs Marion Motley, Jim Brown, and Leroy Kelly; receivers Dante Lavelli, Paul Warfield, and Ozzie Newsome.

Denver Broncos

MAILING ADDRESS: 13655 Broncos Parkway, Englewood, Colorado 80112. **TEAM COLORS:** Orange, royal blue, and white. **PLAYING FIELD:** Mile High Stadium (76,273). **SURFACE:** Grass.

Another original American Football League team in 1960, the Broncos came into the NFL with the merger. Denver was an outstanding AFC team during the 1980s, winning four of five AFC title games. Unfortunately, the Broncos have not fared as well in the Super Bowl; they are one of three teams (Minnesota and Buffalo are the others) to have lost the big game on four different occasions.

Most remembered alumni: Running back Floyd Little; receiver Lionel Taylor; linebackers Randy Gradishar and Tom Jackson; defensive back Louis Wright; kicker Jim Turner.

Houston Oilers

MAILING ADDRESS: 6910 Fannin Street, Houston, Texas 77030. **TEAM COLORS:** Columbia blue, scarlet, and white. **PLAYING FIELD:** Houston Astrodome (62,021). **SURFACE:** AstroTurf-8.

Houston was an original AFL entry in 1960 and the best team in the new league. The Oilers won the first two league titles, the only championships in their history. They have since lost in four AFL/AFC title games and have never reached the Super Bowl.

Most remembered alumni: Quarterbacks George Blanda and Dan Pastorini; running backs Billy Cannon and Earl Campbell; receiver Charley Hennigan; punt returner Billy "White Shoes" Johnson.

Indianapolis Colts

MAILING ADDRESS: P.O. Box 535000, Indianapolis, Indiana 46253. **TEAM COLORS:** Royal blue and white. **PLAYING FIELD:** Hoosier Dome (60,129). **SURFACE:** AstroTurf.

The Colts joined the NFL as the Baltimore Colts in 1953 and within five years were league champions, beating the Giants in sudden-death overtime. The team repeated in 1959, 1968, and 1970. All-told, the Colts have won three NFL titles in four tries. They have split in a pair of AFC title contests and have won a single Super Bowl (Super Bowl V). They were beaten by the New York Jets, 16-7, in Super Bowl III, one of the greatest upsets in football history. The team moved to Indianapolis in 1984.

Most remembered alumni: Quarterbacks John Unitas and Bert Jones; running backs Lenny Moore, Lydell Mitchell, and Alan Ameche; receiver Raymond Berry; linemen Gino Marchetti, Big Daddy Lipscomb, Bubba Smith, Jim Parker, and Art Donovan; defensive back Bobby Boyd; linebacker Mike Curtis.

Kansas City Chiefs

MAILING ADDRESS: One Arrowhead Drive, Kansas City, Missouri 64129. **TEAM COLORS:** Red, gold, and white. **PLAYING FIELD:** Arrowhead Stadium (78,067). **SURFACE:** Grass.

The Chiefs were born as the Dallas Texans with the AFL in 1960. They moved to Kansas City in 1963. The franchise has won three AFC titles, one in Dallas and two in Kansas City. The Chiefs lost the first ever Super Bowl to the Green Bay Packers in 1967. But three years later they came back to win Super Bowl IV in an upset over the Minnesota Vikings.

Most remembered alumni: Quarterback Len Dawson; running back Mike Garrett; receiver Otis Taylor; linemen Jim Tyrer, Jerry Mays, and Buck Buchanan; linebackers Bobby Bell and Willie Lanier; defensive backs Fred "the Hammer" Williamson, Emmitt Thomas, and Johnny Robinson.

Los Angeles Raiders

MAILING ADDRESS: 332 Center Street, El Segundo, California 90245. **TEAM COLORS:** Silver and black. **PLAYING FIELD:** Los Angeles Memorial Coliseum (92,488). **SURFACE:** Grass.

They started in 1960 as the Oakland Raiders, a team that quickly got a reputation for rough play, pride, confidence, and winning. The Raiders were in the second-ever Super Bowl, which they lost to the Green Bay Packers, but then went on to win the big one on three other occasions (Super Bowls XI, XV, XVIII). This successful team, which has been in the AFC title game on 12 occasions, moved to Los Angeles in 1982.

Most remembered alumni: Quarterbacks Daryle Lamonica, George Blanda, Ken Stabler, and Jim Plunkett; running backs Marcus Allen and Bo Jackson; receivers Art Powell, Fred Biletnikoff, Cliff Branch, and Todd Christiansen; linemen Art Shell and Gene Upshaw; defensive end John Matuszak; linebacker Ted Hendricks; defensive backs Willie Brown, George Atkinson, Jack Tatum, and Lester Hayes; punter Ray Guy.

Miami Dolphins

MAILING ADDRESS: Joe Robbie Stadium, 2269 N.W. 199th Street, Miami, Florida 33056. **TEAM COLORS:** Aqua, coral, and white. **PLAYING FIELD:** Joe Robbie Stadium (73,000). **SURFACE:** Grass.

An AFL expansion team in 1966, the Miami Dolphins made the playoffs within five years. Then, in 1972, this seven-year-old franchise became the only NFL team ever to go unbeaten for an entire season—both regular season and playoffs (Miami beat Washington in Super Bowl VII). That was the second of three straight Super Bowl appearances for a team that has made it to the big show five times, winning twice. Miami has had many great individual stars as well as one of pro football's legendary coaches, Don Shula.

Most remembered alumni: Quarterback Bob Griese; running backs Jim Kiick, Larry Csonka, and Mercury Morris; receiver Paul Warfield; linemen Larry Little, Bob Kuechenberg, Jim Langer, and Dwight Stephenson; linebacker Nick Buoniconti; safeties Dick Anderson and Jake Scott.

New England Patriots

MAILING ADDRESS: Route 1, Foxboro, Massachusetts 02035. **TEAM COLORS:** Silver, blue, and red. **PLAYING FIELD:** Foxboro Stadium (60,794). **SURFACE:** Grass.

The Pats, an AFL original in 1960, are a franchise that has been down more than it has been up. The team has made it to a pair of AFC title games, winning one. In their one trip to the Super Bowl (January 1986) they were beaten by the Chicago Bears. As the mid-1990s approach, the club is once again in a rebuilding mode.

Most remembered alumni: Quarterback Steve Grogan; running backs Jim Nance and Sam Cunningham; receiver/placekicker Gino Cappelletti; receiver Stanley Morgan; guard John Hannah.

New York Jets

MAILING ADDRESS: 1000 Fulton Avenue, Hempstead, New York 11550. **TEAM COLORS:** Kelly green and white. **PLAYING FIELD:** Giants Stadium (77,311). **SURFACE:** AstroTurf.

No football fan of the 1960s will ever forget the New York Jets' great upset of the Baltimore Colts in Super Bowl III. The victory put the old AFL on an equal footing with the NFL just before the two leagues merged in 1970. It marked the only appearance of the Jets in the super game. The team, a franchise that has often turned great expectations into disappointment, was in one other AFC title contest and lost.

Most remembered alumni: Quarterback Joe Namath; running backs Matt Snell and Freeman McNeil; receivers Don Maynard and Al Toon; kicker Jim Turner; linemen Randy Rasmussen, John Elliott, Gerry Philbin, and Verlon Biggs.

Pittsburgh Steelers

MAILING ADDRESS: Three Rivers Stadium, 300 Stadium Circle, Pittsburgh, Pennsylvania 15212. **TEAM COLORS:** Black and gold. **PLAYING FIELD:** Three Rivers Stadium (59,600). **SURFACE:** AstroTurf.

The team of the 1970s, the Steelers went all the way in the 1974, 1975, 1978, and 1979 seasons, winning the Super Bowl each time. The team has also played in three additional AFC title games, two of them in the 1970s. Until then, the franchise that had begun back in 1933 had never won a title of any kind. But they more than made up for it with tough, talented teams that played hard and hated to lose.

Most remembered alumni: Quarterbacks Bobby Layne and Terry Bradshaw; running backs John Henry Johnson, Rocky Bleier, and Franco Harris; receivers Lynn Swann and John Stallworth; linemen Mike Webster, Mean Joe Greene, and L.C. Greenwood; linebackers Jack Lambert and Jack Ham; defensive back Mel Blount.

San Diego Chargers

MAILING ADDRESS: Jack Murphy Stadium,
P.O. Box 609609, San Diego, California 92160-9609.
TEAM COLORS: Navy blue, white, and gold.
PLAYING FIELD: San Diego Jack Murphy Stadium
(60,836). **SURFACE:** Grass.

An AFL original, the franchise began play as the Los Angeles Chargers in 1960, moving to San Diego in 1961. The Chargers have been an explosive offensive team during several periods in the franchise's history. The team was in four of the first six AFL title games, winning just once, in 1963. They lost two AFC title games, in 1980 and 1981, and have never traveled to the Super Bowl.

Most remembered alumni: Quarterbacks John Hadl and Dan Fouts; running backs Keith Lincoln and Paul Lowe; receivers Lance Alworth, Gary Garrison, Charlie Joiner, Kellen Winslow, John Jefferson, and Wes Chandler; kick returner Speedy Duncan; linemen Ron Mix and Ernie Ladd; kicker Rolf Benirschke.

Seattle Seahawks

MAILING ADDRESS: 11220 N.E. 53rd Street,
Kirkland, Washington 98033. **TEAM COLORS:** Blue,
green, and silver. **PLAYING FIELD:** Kingdome
(64,400). **SURFACE:** AstroTurf.

One of the two last expansion teams to join the NFL, the Seahawks began play in 1976. The club has been well-represented during several seasons and made it all the way to the AFC title game in 1983 after winning a wild-card spot in the playoffs with a 9-7 record.

Most remembered alumni: Quarterback Jim Zorn; running back Curt Warner; receiver Steve Largent; defensive back Kenny Easley.

NATIONAL FOOTBALL CONFERENCE

Arizona Cardinals

MAILING ADDRESS: P.O. Box 888, Phoenix, Arizona 85001-0888. **TEAM COLORS:** Cardinal red, black, and white. **PLAYING FIELD:** Sun Devil Stadium (73,473). **SURFACE:** Grass.

An old, well-traveled franchise that has often had difficulty winning. The Cardinals joined the American Professional Football Association as a Chicago team in 1920, but they had been a pro franchise long before that. The team moved to St. Louis in 1960, then to Arizona in 1988. Yet the club has won just a single NFL crown, in 1947, and gotten to the title game on just one other occasion, that being in 1948. It's been a long time.

Most remembered alumni: Quarterbacks Jim Hart and Neil Lomax; running backs Ernie Nevers, Charley Trippi, Ollie Matson, and Ottis Anderson; receivers Sonny Randle, Jackie Smith, Roy Green, and J.T. Smith; linemen Ernie McMillan and Dan Dierdorf; linebacker Larry Stalling; defensive backs Larry Wilson and Pat Fischer; kicker Jim Bakken.

Atlanta Falcons

MAILING ADDRESS: 2745 Burnett Road, Suwanee, Georgia 30174. **TEAM COLORS:** Black, red, silver, and white. **PLAYING FIELD:** Georgia Dome (70,500). **SURFACE:** Artificial turf.

An expansion team in 1966, the Falcons have found it difficult rising to the top of the NFC. Winning seasons have been few and far between and last-place finishes are not uncommon. The club has made several trips to the playoffs and took a division crown in 1980. But the Falcons have never been in an NFC title game or, obviously, a Super Bowl.

Most remembered alumni: Quarterback Steve Bartkowski; receiver Alfred Jenkins; kicker Mick Luckhurst; linebacker Tommy Nobis.

Chicago Bears

MAILING ADDRESS: Corporate Headquarters, Halas Hall, 250 North Washington Road, Lake Forest, Illinois 60045. **TEAM COLORS:** Navy blue, orange, and white. **PLAYING FIELD:** Soldier Field (66,946). **SURFACE:** Grass.

In the NFL since 1920, the Monsters of the Midway have been one of the league's most successful franchises. With great players and a great tradition, the Bears have won seven NFL/NFC titles. They have been to the Super Bowl just once, in January 1986, crushing New England, 46-10.

Most remembered alumni: Quarterbacks Sid Luckman and Jim McMahon; running backs Bronko Nagurski, Red Grange, Gale Sayers, and Walter Payton; receivers Mike Ditka and Johnny Morris; linemen Doug Atkins and George Musso; linebackers Dick Butkus and Mike Singletary; defensive back Gary Fencik; owner/coach George Halas.

Dallas Cowboys

MAILING ADDRESS: Cowboys Center, One Cowboys Parkway, Irving, Texas 75063. **TEAM COLORS:** Royal blue, metallic silver blue, and white. **PLAYING FIELD:** Texas Stadium (65,024). **SURFACE:** Texas turf.

America's Team made a dramatic comeback in 1992, ending the season with yet another Super Bowl triumph. They repeated the feat in 1993. An NFL expansion team in 1960, the Cowboys have been one of the league's flagship franchises. The team has been to the Super Bowl seven times, winning four. In addition, the Boys have taken six NFC titles and reached the championship game on seven other occasions.

Most remembered alumni: Coach Tom Landry; quarterbacks Don Meredith and Roger Staubach; running backs Don Perkins, Calvin Hill, and Tony Dorsett; receivers Bob Hayes, Drew Pearson, and Tony Hill; linemen Ralph Neely, Bob Lilly, Randy White, Too Tall Jones, and Harvey Martin; linebackers Jerry Tubbs, Lee Roy Jordan, and Chuck Howley; defensive backs Mel Renfro, Charley Waters, and Cliff Harris.

Detroit Lions

MAILING ADDRESS: Pontiac Silverdome, 1200 Featherstone Road, Pontiac, Michigan 48342. **TEAM COLORS:** Honolulu blue and silver. **PLAYING FIELD:** Pontiac Silverdome (80,500). **SURFACE:** AstroTurf.

The Lions joined the NFL back in 1930 and are a franchise with a great tradition. The Detroit roster, like those of most older NFL franchises, has been filled with great players over the years. Although the Lions have never been to the Super Bowl, the team has four NFL titles in six tries. Their last championship, however, was back in 1957.

Most remembered alumni: Quarterback Bobby Layne; running backs Doak Walker, Howard "Hopalong" Cassady, and Billy Sims; receivers Gail Cogdill, Pat Studstill, and Charlie Sanders; linemen Roger Brown and Alex Karras; linebackers Joe Schmidt, Wayne Walker, and Mike Lucci; defensive backs Yale Lary, Dick LeBeau, and Lem Barney.

Green Bay Packers

MAILING ADDRESS: 1265 Lombardi Avenue, Green Bay, Wisconsin 54307-0628. **TEAM COLORS:** Dark green, gold, and white. **PLAYING FIELDS:** Lambeau Field (59,543); Milwaukee County Stadium (56,051). **SURFACE:** Grass.

Tradition and winning, a combination that extended from the 1920s to the 1970s under legendary coaches Curly Lambeau and Vince Lombardi, have made the Packers one of football's most exciting teams. Playing in the league's smallest city, the Packers have always been big time. The franchise has won eight NFL/NFC championships, more than any other team, and was the winner in the first two Super Bowls, when the pride of the entire league was at stake.

Most remembered alumni: Coaches Lambeau and Lombardi; quarterbacks Arnie Herber and Bart Starr; running backs Paul Hornung and Jim Taylor; receivers Don Hutson, Max McGee, and James Lofton; linemen Forrest Gregg, Jerry Kramer, and Willie Davis; linebackers Ray Nitschke and Dave Robinson; defensive backs Herb Adderley and Willie Wood.

Los Angeles Rams

MAILING ADDRESS: 2327 West Lincoln Avenue, Anaheim, California 92801. **TEAM COLORS:** Royal blue, gold, and white. **PLAYING FIELD:** Anaheim Stadium (69,008). **SURFACE:** Grass.

The Rams franchise started in Cleveland in 1937. The team finally won an NFL title in 1945, then promptly moved to Los Angeles, opening up Cleveland for the Browns. Once in L.A., the Rams won another pair of NFL/NFC titles and made one Super Bowl appearance. More importantly, they reached the NFL/NFC title game on nine other occasions.

Most remembered alumni: Quarterbacks Bob Waterfield and Roman Gabriel; running backs Ollie Matson and Eric Dickerson; receivers Tom Fears, Elroy "Crazylegs" Hirsch, and Harold Jackson; linemen Jackie Slater, Jack Youngblood, and Merlin Olson; linebacker "Hacksaw" Reynolds; defensive backs Eddie Meador and Dick "Night Train" Lane.

Minnesota Vikings

MAILING ADDRESS: 9520 Viking Drive, Eden Prairie, Minnesota 55344. **TEAM COLORS:** Purple, gold, and white. **PLAYING FIELD:** Hubert H. Humphrey Metrodome (63,000).
SURFACE: AstroTurf.

A very successful expansion team, the Vikings joined the NFL in 1961, were winners by 1964, took a divisional crown by 1968, and were in the Super Bowl a year later. All in all, the Vikings have gone to the super game four times. Unfortunately, they share the dubious distinction with the Denver Broncos and the Buffalo Bills of having lost all four. Yet the team has taken four of six NFC championships.

Most remembered alumni: Coach Bud Grant; quarterbacks Fran Tarkenton, Joe Kapp, and Tommy Kramer; running backs Bill Brown and Chuck Foreman; receivers Gene Washington and Ahmad Rashad; linemen Ron Yary, Ed White, Carl Eller, Alan Page, and Jim Marshall; defensive back Paul Krause.

New Orleans Saints

MAILING ADDRESS: 1500 Poydras Street, New Orleans, Louisiana 70112. **TEAM COLORS:** Old gold, black, and white. **PLAYING FIELD:** Louisiana Superdome (69,065). **SURFACE:** AstroTurf.

Like the Atlanta Falcons, the New Orleans Saints have found it difficult building from expansion in 1967. Finally, in the late 1980s and early 1990s the team became competitive. The Saints won a divisional title in 1991, but the club has never made it to the NFC championship game or Super Bowl. And, boy, did those early players take their lumps.

Most remembered alumni: Quarterback Archie Manning; running backs George Rogers and Tony Galbreath; receiver Wes Chandler; defensive backs Tom Myers and Dave Waymer; kicker Tom Dempsey.

New York Giants

MAILING ADDRESS: Giants Stadium, East Rutherford, New Jersey 07073. **TEAM COLORS:** Blue, red, and white. **PLAYING FIELD:** Giants Stadium (77,311). **SURFACE:** AstroTurf.

Yet another glorious old franchise, begun in 1925 and finding success in almost each decade. The Giants have been in more NFL/NFC title games than any other franchise, winning five of the 16 in which they played. But Super Bowl championships at the end of the 1986 and 1990 seasons were the team's first titles since back in 1956, a long wait.

Most remembered alumni: Quarterbacks Charlie Conerly and Y. A. Tittle; running backs Tuffy Leemans, Frank Gifford, Ron Johnson, and Joe Morris; receivers Del Shofner, Homer Jones, and Mark Bavaro; linemen Mel Hein, Roosevelt Brown, Andy Robustelli, and Roosevelt Grier; linebackers Sam Huff and Lawrence Taylor; defensive backs Emlen Tunnell and Jim Patton; kicker Pat Summerall.

Philadelphia Eagles

MAILING ADDRESS: 3501 South Broad Street, Philadelphia, Pennsylvania 19148. **TEAM COLORS:** Kelly green, silver, and white. **PLAYING FIELD:** Veterans Stadium (65,178). **SURFACE:** AstroTurf-8.

Like many other NFC teams, the Eagles go back a long way. Philly began NFL play in 1933. Despite 60 years in the league, the team has won only four NFL/NFC titles, going to the Super Bowl one time, in January 1981. But the Eagles have often been competitive and have produced a number of outstanding players.

Most remembered alumni: Quarterbacks Tommy Thompson, Norm Van Brocklin, and Sonny Jurgensen; running backs Steve Van Buren and Wilbert Montgomery; receivers Pete Phihos, Pete Retzlaff, Tommy McDonald, and Harold Carmichael; lineman Carl Hairston; linebacker Bill Bergey; defensive back Bill Bradley.

San Francisco 49ers

MAILING ADDRESS: 4949 Centennial Boulevard, Santa Clara, California 95054-1229. **TEAM COLORS:** Forty Niners gold and scarlet. **PLAYING FIELD:** Candlestick Park (66,513). **SURFACE:** Grass.

The team of the 1980s, the Niners dominated opponents to the tune of four Super Bowl victories at the end of the 1981, 1984, 1988, and 1989 seasons. Originally a member of the old All-America Conference, the Niners came into the NFL in 1950 but struggled until 1970, when they finally made it to the NFC title game. They lost to Dallas that year and the next year as well, before starting their remarkable run 10 years later. San Francisco has also been the home of many great individual stars.

Most remembered alumni: Quarterbacks Y. A. Tittle, John Brodie, and Joe Montana; running backs Joe "the Jet" Perry, Hugh McElhenny, and Roger Craig; receivers Bernie Casey and Dwight Clark; linemen Leo Nomellini, Bob St. Clair, Forrest Blue, and Randy Cross; defensive backs Abe Woodson, Jimmy Johnson, and Ronnie Lott.

Tampa Bay Buccaneers

MAILING ADDRESS: One Buccaneer Place, Tampa, Florida 33607. **TEAM COLORS:** Florida orange, white, and red. **PLAYING FIELD:** Tampa Stadium (74,292). **SURFACE:** Grass.

One of the last two expansion teams to enter the NFL in 1976, the Buccaneers have had problems sustaining a winning tradition. After a 0-14 opening season, the Bucs turned it around and won a division title just three years later, making it to the NFC title game. But winning seasons have been few and far between since. The Bucs continue to look for the right formula for sustained success.

Most remembered alumni: Quarterback Doug Williams; running backs Ricky Bell and James Wilder; receivers Kevin House and Jimmie Giles; lineman Lee Roy Selmon; linebacker Hugh Green.

Washington Redskins

MAILING ADDRESS: P.O. Box 17247, Dulles International Airport, Washington, D.C. 20041. **TEAM COLORS:** Burgundy and gold. **PLAYING FIELD:** Robert F. Kennedy Memorial Stadium (55,677). **SURFACE:** Grass.

The Skins came into the NFL in 1932 and found their first period of success when quarterback Sammy Baugh joined the team in 1937. Great individual players and a winning tradition have prevailed ever since. Washington has won seven NFL/NFC titles in 12 tries, and taken the Super Bowl championship three times in five trips. "Hail to the Redskins" is one of the most recognizable fight songs in the league.

Most remembered alumni: Coaches George Allen and Joe Gibbs; quarterbacks Sammy Baugh, Sonny Jurgensen, Billy Kilmer, and Joe Theismann; running backs Larry Brown and John Riggins; receivers Bobby Mitchell and Charley Taylor; linemen Joe Rutgens, Len Hauss, and Dexter Manley; linebackers Chris Hanburger and Jack Pardee; defensive backs Ken Houston, Joe Lavender, Lemar Parrish, and Mark Murphy; kicker Mark Moseley.

1995 EXPANSION TEAMS

Carolina Panthers

MAILING ADDRESS: 227 West Trade Street, Charlotte, North Carolina 28202. **TEAM COLORS:** Silver, blue, and black. **PLAYING FIELD:** Carolina Stadium (under construction, 72,300). **SURFACE:** Grass.

On October 26, 1993, the NFL awarded an expansion franchise to the Carolina Panthers. The Panthers, based in Charlotte, North Carolina, became the first new team to join the NFL since 1976, and the first of two expansion teams added in 1993. Carolina is the NFL's 29th team, and is scheduled to begin play in 1995.

Jacksonville Jaguars

MAILING ADDRESS: One Stadium Place, Jacksonville, Florida 32202. **TEAM COLORS:** Teal, gold, and black. **PLAYING FIELD:** The Gator Bowl (renovation will reduce seating to 73,000). **SURFACE:** Grass.

The Jacksonville Jaguars became the second of the two NFL expansion teams added in 1993, as well as the league's 30th team, when they were awarded a franchise on November 30, 1993. The Jaguars are scheduled to begin play in 1995.

4

Some
Amazing
NFL Records

Here are some of the most amazing records ever set in the National Football League. You might be too young to remember most of them, but if you're a football fan you'll know right away how tough they were to set and why they've lasted so long.

NEVERS SCORES AND SCORES AND SCORES AND....

Ernie Nevers was typical of the old-time football players. He was tough, talented, and tireless, a guy who hated to come out of a game, even for a minute. When Nevers played in the 1920s, no one wore facemasks, and helmets and pads did not provide much protection. Nevers, a star for Stanford University, was such an enthusiastic player that Notre Dame coach Knute Rockne once described him as "fury in football boots."

By 1929, Nevers was 26 years old and the player/coach of the NFL Chicago Cardinals. On November 28, Thanksgiving Day, the Cardinals met the crosstown Bears on an icy field at Comiskey Park. There were only about 8,000 fans brave enough to watch on that bitter cold day, but what they saw made NFL history.

In the first quarter Nevers ran 10 yards for the first score of the game. He was also the kicker, but missed the extra point. Minutes later his club drove again, and this time he bulled his way in from five yards out. His kick brought the score to 13-0. Then in the second quarter he scored from the six and booted the point, putting Chicago ahead at 20-0.

After halftime, Nevers was at it again. He blasted over from the one and scored his fifth TD on another short plunge early in the fourth quarter. Minutes later, the big fullback scored his sixth and final TD on another powerful, 10-yard burst. His final extra point gave the Cards a 40-6 victory.

Nevers's six TDs and four extra points, 40 points in all, remains the all-time record for the most points scored in one game. It is also the oldest individual mark in the NFL record book.

SLINGIN' SAM HAD A LEG, TOO

Slingin' Sammy Baugh will always be remembered as pro football's first great passing quarterback. While the Texas native set a number of passing records during his 16-year NFL career, he also set another record that is largely forgotten.

Besides starring at quarterback, Baugh was also the Washington Redskins' punter. And, boy, could he kick. He was particularly adept at the quick kick, taking a direct snap from center and surprising the defense by booting the ball after just one quick step. He once quick-kicked the football 83 yards.

Despite the influx of great punters in recent years—the likes of Jerrel Wilson, Dave Jennings, Ray Guy, and others—it is Sammy Baugh who still holds two great punting marks.

In 1940, Sammy booted the ball 35 times for 1,799 yards. That's an average of 51.4 yards a punt, not only giving Baugh the best single season average ever, but making him the only punter in NFL history to average more than 50 yards for a season.

But that isn't all. Punting the ball 338 times during his career (a lot less than punters today), Baugh compiled a 45.1 average, the best in the history of the National Football League. Who said Slingin' Sam could only throw?

BUT, OH, COULD HE EVER THROW

Don't be too quick to overlook Sammy Baugh's passing. Although many of his records have been broken, a few still stand. For example, he led the league in passing on six different occasions. Now you might say that today's quarterbacks are so good that the competition to lead the league is more intense. Perhaps.

But Baugh set a passing record that no one has been able to top in more than 40 years. Leading the Redskins against the old Boston Braves on October 31, 1948, Baugh completed one long pass after another. When the game ended, he had completed 24 passes and gained 446 yards. That's a record average gain of 18.58 yards a pass! No pro quarterback since has had that kind of explosive game.

To show the greatness of that mark, the quarterbacks who came closest to topping Sam were a couple of pretty fair Sunday signal-callers—John Unitas and Joe Namath.

FEATHERS FLYING

For years the measuring stick for NFL running backs has been the 1,000-yard mark. Gain 1,000 yards in a season and a runner has had a big year. In recent years, with the NFL schedule going from 12 to 14, and now to 16 games, the 1,000-yard touchstone has been diminished somewhat. But it's still a standard a runner can be proud to achieve.

Back in the 1930s, running backs did not get as many carries as they do today. But in 1934, each time Chicago Bears rookie Beattie Feathers carried the ball, he seemed to do something special with it. Feathers twisted, turned, faked, sprinted, darted, spun, and worked for every single yard he could get.

When the season ended, Feathers had gained 1,004 yards, becoming the first man in NFL annals to reach that milestone. That mark, of course, has long been broken. But what makes Feathers's achievement so extraordinary is that he did it while carrying the ball just 101 times! That's an average of 9.94 yards per carry, a single-season mark that stands to this day.

It would take 13 more seasons before another runner cracked the 1,000-yard barrier. And when the great Steve Van Buren finally did it in 1947, it took him 217 carries to gain 1,008 yards. No one has done it quite like Beattie Feathers.

LUCKMAN WINGS IT

Sid Luckman was the first T-formation quarterback, starring with the powerful Chicago Bears in the 1940s. Perhaps best remembered for his epic duels against Sammy Baugh and the Redskins, Luckman nevertheless wrote some football history of his own.

It happened on November 14, 1943, when Luckman and the Monsters of the Midway hit the road to meet to the New York Giants. It didn't take Luckman long before he unleashed his accurate right arm. Early in the contest he fired a touchdown pass to Jim Benton. Then late in the second quarter he whistled a second scoring pass to Cornelius Berry.

Early in the second half, Luckman went back to work and fired one to Hampton Pool in the New York end zone. TD toss number four was a 33-yarder to Harry Clark. But Luckman wasn't through yet. With his eye set on Baugh's record of six TD passes, Luckman threw his fifth to Jim Benton, then a sixth to George Wilson. He had tied his rival's record.

With just seconds left in the game, Luckman dropped back and went deep to Hampton Pool. The fleet receiver grabbed the ball with his fingertips as he crossed the goal line. The Bears won the game,

56-7, as Luckman set a new record with seven touchdown passes. It's a mark that has since been tied by several NFL quarterbacks, but Luckman has a share of the record he set in an era when the pass was just coming into its own.

THE DUTCHMAN GOES DEEP

Another great passing mark that has stood the test of time came from the arm of Norm Van Brocklin. The Dutchman, as he was called, joined the Los Angeles Rams in 1949, splitting time with the Rams' other great signal-caller, Bob Waterfield. But Van Brocklin was in there for the opening game of the 1951 season and got such a hot hand that he stayed in.

With a pair of All-Pro receivers in Tom Fears and Elroy "Crazylegs" Hirsch, Van Brocklin made it look easy. Hirsch grabbed TD throws covering 46, 47, and 26 yards, and another that was a mere one yard. Halfback Verda "Vitamin T" Smith was on the end of a 67-yard Van Brocklin scoring pass.

When the game ended, the Rams had an easy victory, 54-14, and Norm Van Brocklin had made NFL history. The Dutchman had completed 27 of 41 passes for five touchdowns. A great day in any

league. The result of those completions was a record-setting 554 yards gained, the most yardage picked up in a single day by any NFL quarterback. It's a record that still stands. The Dutchman is in the Hall of Fame now, voted in because of an excellent, overall career. But on one afternoon in 1949 he threw for more yards than any of the great ones, before or since.

NO POCKETS PICKED HERE

Even the best and most careful quarterbacks will be intercepted now and then. They might be gambling late in a game, or just have a pass tipped, then picked off. A receiver might slip and fall, opening the lane up for a defensive back. There are numerous ways passes can be stolen.

**Green Bay Packers
quarterback Bart Starr**

That's why the record set by quarterback Bart Starr of the Green Bay Packers was so impressive. Starr was a smart and decisive quarterback who led the great Packer teams of the early and mid-1960s. Playing under Coach Vince Lombardi, Starr directed an attack that used the run to set up the pass. And when he passed the football, Bart Starr was extremely accurate and rarely intercepted.

But he outdid himself during the 1964 and 1965 seasons when he threw an amazing 294 straight passes without suffering an interception. He obliterated the old record and some said his mark would never be broken.

For 25 years, it wasn't. Then along came Bernie Kosar of the Cleveland Browns. Kosar was a sidearm thrower who didn't have an explosive arm and was slow of foot. But, like Starr, he was an extremely intelligent quarterback with a great feel for the passing game. In 1991 Kosar came out throwing. He threw and threw, and then he threw some more. And no one was picking off his passes.

With Starr's record in sight, Kosar kept throwing. Sure enough, he topped it. In fact, Bernie threw his first 308 passes of the season before finally suffering an interception. He was proud of his new record.

"To go this long without an interception in the NFL you've got to have some breaks," he said. "And for us to be competitive, I just can't afford to make mistakes."

For 308 straight passes, he didn't.

THE LONGEST FOOT

Today's field-goal kickers are better than ever. Almost all of the modern field-goal kickers use the soccer style, approaching the ball from an angle. It makes for more distance and accuracy. Yet one of the great kicking records in the NFL was set more than 20 years ago by an old-fashioned straight-ahead kicker who, amazingly, had just half a foot.

He was Tom Dempsey who, in 1970, was the booter for the New Orleans Saints. Dempsey was born without a right hand and with only half a right foot, his kicking foot. Yet he made himself into a fine athlete. Besides being a placekicker, Dempsey was a defensive end, shot-putter, and wrestler in college. He later played tackle and linebacker in the Atlantic Coast Football League. But in the NFL he was strictly a kicker, and a good one. He wore a special square shoe on his kicking foot.

Tom Dempsey of the Saints kicks his way into NFL history with a 63-yard field goal, November 8, 1970.

Dempsey made NFL history on November 8, 1970, when the Saints hosted the Detroit Lions. Oddly enough, he was in a kicking slump at the time. But the game was close and with just 18 seconds left Detroit's Errol Mann kicked an 18-yard field goal to give the Lions a 17-16 lead. The Saints ran the kickoff back to their own 28, then quarterback Billy Kilmer hit Al Dodd with a pass at the 45. But there were just two seconds left.

Onto the field trotted Tom Dempsey. He would be booting from the 37, a distance of 63 yards from the goalposts.

"I knew I could kick it 63 yards," said Dempsey, "but I wasn't sure I could kick it straight."

The ball was snapped and placed down. Dempsey stepped straight into it and swung his right leg in a short but powerful arc. The ball rocketed off the ground and toward the goalposts. Players on both teams stared in disbelief. The kick was up … and good! Tom Dempsey's incredible field goal had not only won the game for the Saints, but set an NFL distance record that has never been broken.

LUCKY 7 FOR BAKKEN

Like Tom Dempsey, Jim Bakken of the old St. Louis Cardinals was one of a dying breed of straight-ahead field-goal kickers. Bakken was an outstanding athlete who practiced at wide receiver during the week, but the Cards didn't want to play him there because of the risk of injury. He was too valuable to them as a kicker.

He really proved it on September 24, 1967, when the Cards met the Pittsburgh Steelers at Pitt Stadium. Bakken and all the other old-style kickers were aware that a soccer-style kicker named Garo Yepremian had set a new record by booting six field goals in a game a year earlier. And on this September day, Jim Bakken didn't feel quite right.

"In practice, I didn't feel my leg was as strong as usual," he said, "and the wind was really playing tricks with the ball."

In the first period, Bakken came on to boot field goals of 18 and 24 yards. Then early in the second session he barely missed a 50-yarder. But he came back to connect on a 33-yard effort. Before the half, Bakken hit on a 29-yarder, his fourth three-pointer of the game. The Cards led, 19-7.

Bakken missed a 45-yarder in the third quarter, but early in the fourth he hit a 24-yarder. Then, with 5:33 left, he connected from 32 yards for his sixth field goal of the game, tying Yepremian's record. In the closing seconds, Bakken got his last chance. With the butterflies churning in his stomach, he split the uprights from 23 yards away to set a new record. Seven field goals in a game. It hasn't been done in a regulation game since.

On November 5, 1989, however, Rich Karlis of the Minnesota Vikings kicked seven field goals in seven attempts in a game against the Los Angeles Rams, connecting on kicks of 20, 24, 22, 25, 29, 36, and 40 yards. Although the game went into overtime, Karlis kicked all seven of his field goals in regulation time. Minnesota won the game on a safety, 23-21. This was the first and, so far, only time in NFL history that an overtime game has been decided by a safety.

THE JUICE SETS 'EM, OTHERS BREAK 'EM

There's little doubt that O. J. Simpson was one of the most electrifying runners of all time. He was an unsurpassed tailback at the University of Southern California (USC), then became a record setter with the Buffalo Bills of the NFL. It started in 1973 when the Juice began churning out yardage at an incredible pace. In the opener against New England he exploded for touchdown runs of 80 and 22 yards, winding up with a single-game record of 250 yards.

O. J. went from there. In the final two games of the season he rambled for 219 yards against New England and 200 yards against the New York Jets to become the first runner in NFL history to gain more than 2,000 yards in a season. He finished with 2,003 yards on 332 carries in 14 games.

The record stood until 1984, when Rams second-year running back Eric Dickerson ran for 2,105 yards on 379 carries in 16 games. Dickerson had two games of 200-plus yards and another of 191. Some feel O. J.'s achievement was more significant because he did it in two fewer games. But both men were great backs and Dickerson now has the record.

In 1976, three years after setting the season record, the Juice broke his own single-game record when he rambled for 273 yards against Detroit. But that same season it was Walter Payton, a second-year halfback in Chicago, who led the NFL in rushing.

A year later, in 1977, Payton was better than ever. He showed the entire football world what he was made of on November 20, when the

Bears played the Minnesota Vikings. Before the game Payton felt weak and listless. He was suffering from the flu but decided to give it a try.

Suddenly he was churning out the yardage, twisting and turning, using his power and his speed to break tackle after tackle. As the game went on, he seemed to get stronger and the offense kept calling his number.

When the game ended, Walter Payton had set a new single-game record by gaining 275 yards on 40 carries. The Bears won, 10-7, and afterward reporters asked Payton about his health.

"If the game had gone into overtime, I imagine I could have gone some more," Walter said.

The mark of a great football player, without a doubt.

5

More
Amazing
NFL Records

S ince the list of great
achievements in the
NFL is nearly endless,
here's a quick look
at some of the other
records set by the
game's top players
over the years.

Sammy Baugh

That man again. In addition to his numerous passing records, Slingin' Sam set a unique mark on November 14, 1943. That day Baugh's Redskins topped the Lions, 42-20, with Sammy throwing for four touchdowns. But back then, Baugh was a 60-minute man, playing defense, too. Not only did he throw four touchdown passes, but he intercepted four passes as well! Don't expect that one to be broken.

George Halas

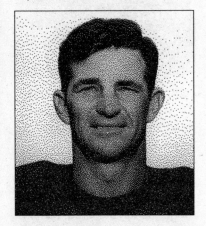

George Halas

The man known as "Papa Bear" had an unusual distinction. He not only founded and owned the Chicago Bears, he coached the team as well. Not content to sit and watch, Halas stayed behind the bench for 40 icy Chicago winters, guiding his beloved Bears. That's longer than any other coach in NFL history.

Lenny Moore

A versatile halfback/wide receiver with the Baltimore Colts during their heyday in the late 1950s and early 1960s, the explosive Moore set a mark that stands to this day. From the end of 1963 through early 1965, he scored at least one touchdown in 18 consecutive games.

John Unitas

A teammate of Lenny Moore, Johnny U. came out of the sandlots to lead the Colts to a pair of titles in the late 1950s. Still called the best ever by many, Unitas set a record that is often compared with Joe DiMaggio's 56-game hitting streak in baseball. Between 1956 and 1960, Unitas threw at least one touchdown pass in 47 consecutive games. Amazing.

Tom Fears

A Hall of Fame receiver with the Los Angeles Rams, Tom Fears set a record that has never been broken. In a game against the Packers on December 3, 1950, Fears grabbed an incredible 18 passes from Rams quarterbacks Bob Waterfield and Norm Van Brocklin. He gained 189 yards and scored twice as the Rams won, 51-14.

George Blanda

Football's grand old man played 26 years in the AFL and NFL as a quarterback and placekicker, a record in itself. But Blanda holds yet another mark. He wound up scoring 2,002 points in his career, 303 points more than runner-up Jan Stenerud. Blanda did it with a mix of nine touchdowns, 943 extra points and 335 field goals. Another record that will be tough to beat.

Miami Dolphins

In 1972 the Dolphins set an NFL mark that still hasn't been topped. Coach Don Shula's ballclub went through the regular 14-game season and the playoffs unbeaten, the only unbeaten and untied team in NFL history. That's 17 straight wins, culminating in a Super Bowl championship. Quite a feat.

Dan Marino

The great quarterback of the Miami Dolphins could end up the all-time leader in many passing categories. He has already set a number of records including the most touchdown passes in a season. Marino fired 48 scoring strikes in 1984, the same year he became the only quarterback in NFL history to pass for more than 5,000 yards, topping out at 5,084.

Warren Moon

A passing master with the Houston Oilers, Warren Moon

holds the NFL mark for passes attempted and completed in a single season. In 1991 Moon threw an amazing 655 passes, completing 404 of them. But Warren could always throw. Before coming to the NFL he played six years in Canada and in 1983 passed for a pro football record of 5,648 yards!

Joe Montana

The man many call the best quarterback of all time, Joe

Montana has set a number of NFL records. As of 1993, he was the highest-rated passer in pro football history and had led the San Francisco 49ers to four Super Bowl titles. Always a smart and accurate passer, Montana set a 1987 mark by completing 22 passes in a row.

Jim Marshall

A defensive end who played one year with the Cleveland Browns and then 19 with the Minnesota Vikings, Marshall was always an outstanding player. But he is also remembered for his durability. Battling in the trenches for 20 NFL seasons, Jim Marshall never missed a game, playing in 282 consecutive contests, 42 more than his nearest rival.

Jim Brown

The standout fullback of the Cleveland Browns in the 1950s and 1960s, Jim Brown is still thought of as the greatest running back in pro football history. The fact that many of his records have been broken doesn't diminish his accomplishments. To show how Brown dominated his era, he still holds the record for leading the league in rushing. Jim topped all runners in eight of his nine seasons in the NFL.

Sterling Sharpe

An outstanding receiver with the Green Bay Packers, Sterling Sharpe has a knack for getting into the clear and coming up with the big catch. In 1992 he did it more often and better than any other receiver in history. Sharpe grabbed 108 passes for the season, topping the 106 catches by Washington's Art Monk, set eight years earlier. A year later in 1993, Sharpe was even better. He broke his own record by catching 112 passes for the season.

Phil Simms

Widely considered one of the better quarterbacks in the National Football League, Phil Simms picked the sport's biggest stage on which to shine his brightest. In Super Bowl XXI on January 25, 1987, Simms led the New York Giants to a 39-20 victory over the Denver Broncos. In doing so, the New York QB put on a record-breaking passing exhibition, completing an amazing 22 of 25 passes, an 88 percent success rate. And two of the three misses were dropped.

Paul Hornung

Green Bay's "Golden Boy" halfback of the 1950s and 1960s, Paul Hornung was a genuine triple threat. He could run, pass,

and kick. He showed it all in 1960 when he ran for 15 touchdowns, and kicked 15 field goals and 41 extra points for 176 points, an NFL single-season scoring record. Not too many players can do it all the way Hornung could.

Walter Payton

Walter Payton must have been born to run with a football, because he carried the ball more than any other back in NFL history. Playing his entire 13-year career with the Chicago Bears, Payton carried the ball a record 3,838 times, gained more than 1,000 yards a record 10 seasons, ran for a record 110 touchdowns, and retired with a record 16,726 yards gained rushing. No other player comes close.

Timmy Smith

Perhaps one of the least-known record breakers ever, Timmy Smith was a rookie substitute who took over at fullback for the Washington Redskins in Super Bowl XXII. Running against the Denver Broncos, Smith led Washington to victory by gaining a record 204 yards on 22 carries. It was a one-shot deal, as Smith never won a regular job in the NFL again.

Chicago Bears

The Bears' long history features a multitude of highlights and records. But perhaps no mark is more amazing than the team's victory over the Washington Redskins in the NFL title game of 1940. It was a day when everything went right for the Bears and wrong for the Redskins. Chicago simply blasted the Skins by the most one-sided championship score in history, 73-0.

6

NFL
Championship
Games, 1933-1966

Prior to 1933, the National Football League had just one division, thus no championship game. The team with the best regular-season mark was declared the champion. Then, in 1933, the league split into two divisions and added a title game. It became football's biggest contest until the start of the Super Bowl in January 1967.

Here is a brief rundown of each National Football League championship game, with some important highlights.

1933 **Chicago Bears** 23 **New York Giants** 21

The great Chicago fullback Bronko Nagurski threw two option passes for touchdowns. Jack Manders booted three field goals for the Bears.

1934 **New York Giants** 30 **Chicago Bears** 13

Sweet revenge. Famous "sneakers" game. Giants donned sneakers on frozen field in fourth quarter and scored 27 unanswered points to win the game.

1935 **Detroit Lions** 26 **New York Giants** 7

A small crowd led to a winner's share of just $313.35 per man. The losers took home $200.20 each. Compare that to today's purses.

1936 **Green Bay Packers** 21 **Boston Redskins** 6

Packer QB Arnie Herber threw a 50-yard TD pass to the great receiver Don Hutson.

1937 **Washington Redskins** 28 **Chicago Bears** 21

A great rivalry began as Skins rookie quarterback Sammy Baugh threw three long TD passes.

1938 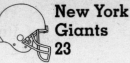 New York Giants 23   Green Bay Packers 17

Five injured Giants all insisted on playing. After the victory, two of them had to be hospitalized. Talk about tough.

1939 Green Bay Packers 27   New York Giants 0

What a difference a year makes. Packers scored 20 points in the second half to ensure the victory.

1940 Chicago Bears 73   Washington Redskins 0

And to think the same two teams played a 7-3 game during the regular season, Washington winning. Some payback, huh?

1941 Chicago Bears 37   New York Giants 9

It was 28-3 after intermission as the Bears rushed for 192 yards and scored four touchdowns. Monsters of the Midway for sure.

1942 Washington Redskins 14   Chicago Bears 6

Bears were 11-0 in regular season but Sammy Baugh spun his magic again.

1943 Chicago Bears **41** Washington Redskins **21**

Seems like the same few teams every year. Sid Luckman of the Bears threw for five TDs in this one. Baugh nailed a pair.

1944 Green Bay Packers **14** New York Giants **7**

Giants lineman Al Blozis played while on a pass from his army unit. A month later he was killed in action during the Battle of the Bulge.

1945 Cleveland Rams **15** Washington Redskins **14**

The Rams in pre-Los Angeles days won their first title behind rookie quarterback Bob Waterfield.

1946 Chicago Bears **24** New York Giants **14**

Sid Luckman dominated again, scoring the winning touchdown on a 19-yard bootleg play in the fourth quarter.

1947 Chicago Cardinals **28** Philadelphia Eagles **21**

Chicago's "other" team, led by the versatile Charley Trippi, won by rushing for 282 yards.

1948 **Philadelphia Eagles 7** **Chicago Cardinals 0**

This one was played in a near blizzard with Philly's Steve Van Buren scoring the only touchdown from the five.

1949 **Philadelphia Eagles 14** **Los Angeles Rams 0**

For the second year in a row, Philadelphia blanked its rival with an amazing performance by Steve Van Buren, who gained 196 yards on 31 carries in heavy rain and mud.

1950 **Cleveland Browns 30** **Los Angeles Rams 28**

In their first-ever NFL season the Browns won a great game on a Lou Groza 16-yard field goal with just 28 seconds remaining. A classic.

1951 **Los Angeles Rams 24** **Cleveland Browns 17**

The Browns were 11-1 in the regular season, but L.A.'s Tom Fears caught a 73-yard TD bomb from Norm Van Brocklin for the game winner.

1952 **Detroit Lions 17** **Cleveland Browns 7**

A 67-yard run by Detroit halfback Doak Walker broke the backs of the Browns.

1953 **Detroit Lions 17** **Cleveland Browns 16**

Three title-game losses in a row for the powerful Browns. Lions QB Bobby Layne threw for a clutch, 33-yard score to receiver Jim Doran.

1954 **Cleveland Browns 56** **Detroit Lions 10**

Cleveland's great quarterback Otto Graham threw for three touchdowns and ran for two more as the Browns romped.

1955 **Cleveland Browns 38** **Los Angeles Rams 14**

Six straight title game appearances for the Browns. Dynasty anyone? In Otto Graham's final game he tossed two TD passes and scored two more TDs on short runs. A true leader.

1956 **New York Giants 47** **Chicago Bears 7**

A blowout. Everything went right for Giants' defense, and for offensive standouts Conerly, Gifford, Rote, Alex Webster, and Ben Agajanian.

1957 **Detroit Lions 59** **Cleveland Browns 14**

Lions won big despite presence of Cleveland rookie runner Jim Brown. Detroit's Tobin Rote threw for four scores.

1958 **Baltimore Colts** 23   **New York Giants** 17

The first "sudden-death" overtime title game. Alan "the Horse" Ameche scored game winner in a contest that many still call greatest game ever.

1959 **Baltimore Colts** 31   **New York Giants** 16

Too much Johnny Unitas. The Colts' great QB completed 18 of 29 for 265 yards and two scores. Anticlimax from 1958 game.

1960 **Philadelphia Eagles** 17   **Green Bay Packers** 13

Packers, on rise under Lombardi, fell a little bit short. Eagles' Norm Van Brocklin quarterbacked his final game to go out a winner.

1961 **Green Bay Packers** 37   **New York Giants** 0

Packer dynasty served notice it had arrived. Bart Starr threw for three scores and Pack offense rushed for 181 yards. Lombardi football.

1962 **Green Bay Packers** 16   **New York Giants** 7

Four title-game losses in five years for Giants. The Packers' defense was becoming a dominating unit.

1963  Chicago Bears **14** New York Giants **10**

Eight-degree weather hurt the New York passing game as five interceptions propelled Bears to yet another title.

1964 Cleveland Browns **27** Baltimore Colts **0**

Three Frank Ryan to Gary Collins TD passes sealed the Colts' fate. Unitas didn't have any miracles left in this one.

1965 Green Bay Packers **23** Cleveland Browns **12**

In a game played on a slushy field, the Packer line play and ground game dominated. Packers controlled the ball most of second half.

1966 Green Bay Packers **34** Dallas Cowboys **27**

Winner of this would go to first-ever Super Bowl. Cowboys, the new kids on the block, put up gallant fight. Last-second goal-line stand saved the game for the Packers.

After 1966, the NFL title games lost some significance as the Super Bowl grew in importance. After the complete merger of the NFL and AFL in 1970, the Super Bowl became the only real championship game in town.

AFL CHAMPIONSHIP GAMES
1960-1966

The American Football League was formed with two divisions in 1960. Like the NFL, the AFL held a yearly championship game that became less important after the first Super Bowl. Here is a brief rundown of the first seven AFL title contests.

1960 **Houston Oilers 24**   **Los Angeles Chargers 16**

Quarterback George Blanda threw for three scores, including an 88-yarder to Billy Cannon as Oilers win first-ever AFL title.

1961 **Houston Oilers 10**   **San Diego Chargers 3**

The Chargers, now a San Diego team, still went down to defeat. Blanda hit Cannon from 35 yards out for the only touchdown of the game.

1962 **Dallas Texans 20**   **Houston Oilers 17**

A double overtime thriller with Tommy Brooker kicking the winning field goal from the 25. Oilers had scored 17 second-half points to tie.

1963 **San Diego Chargers 51**   **Boston Patriots 10**

Chargers' Keith Lincoln ran for 206 yards. San Diego offense, led by Lincoln, halfback Paul Lowe, and receiver Lance Alworth, was awesome.

1964 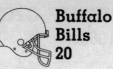 **Buffalo Bills 20** **San Diego Chargers 7**

Bills quarterbacked by Jack Kemp, who went on to become a U.S. congressman and then a member of President George Bush's Cabinet. Buffalo fullback Cookie Gilchrist ran for 122 yards to control game.

1965 **Buffalo Bills 23** **San Diego Chargers 0**

Two in a row for the Bills. Soccer-style placekicker Pete Gogolak booted three field goals.

1966 **Kansas City Chiefs 31** **Buffalo Bills 7**

Winner would go to first-ever Super Bowl. Quarterback Len Dawson and halfback Mike Garrett led an explosive Kansas City offense.

With the AFL growing in stature and talent, and a price war for top players harming both leagues, a merger of the two leagues was announced in 1966. Some interleague games were scheduled starting in 1967, with the full merger coming in 1970.

The Super Bowl

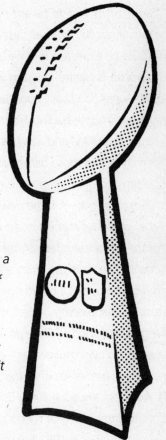

The first Super Bowl game was a curiosity more than anything else. It marked the first time that an established National Football League team met a team from the upstart American Football League. In fact the game, played on January 15, 1967, wasn't even called the Super Bowl. It was billed as the AFL-NFL World Championship Game.

The term "super bowl," in fact, has a history of its own. Lamar Hunt, one of the AFL founders and owner of the Kansas City Chiefs, came home one night to find his young daughter playing with a ball. When he asked what it was, she replied, "This is my super ball, daddy."

The phrase stuck in Hunt's mind. Slowly, it changed to super bowl, and he began mentioning it at meetings. Once the other owners began to use it, the press picked up on it. The rest, as they say, is history.

There was a great deal of pride at stake when the first Super Bowl game was played. Vince Lombardi's aging Green Bay Packers were the NFL champs and they felt they were playing with the pride of the entire league on their shoulders. The AFL champs, the Kansas City Chiefs, wanted to prove that their league could compete with the NFL.

The first Super Bowl game set a precedent. It was played at the Los Angeles Memorial Coliseum. Some felt it should have been played at the host NFL city, Green Bay. But Green Bay is often frigid in January and league officials didn't want the weather to be a major factor in the game's final results. After all, a team used to playing in the cold and snow could be expected to have a definite advantage over a team that plays most of its games in warm weather.

So the Super Bowl has almost always been played at a neutral site (in neither team's home stadium) in the southern part of the United States. Only Super Bowls XVI and XXVI, in 1982 and 1992, were played in northern cities. But those games were indoors: at the Pontiac Silverdome in Michigan and the Hubert H. Humphrey Metrodome in Minnesota. The 1993 game was played at the new Georgia Dome in Atlanta.

In the early days many argued that playing at a neutral site wasn't fair for the hometown fans. After all, they had followed their team all year and should have the chance to see it in the Super Bowl. This was a sound argument, but it could not overcome the image of the sport's greatest spectacle being played in the subzero weather of Green Bay, or the cold and wind of Chicago, or the sleet and ice of New England or New York. A warm-weather—or indoor—site it would be.

Here, then, are recaps of all the Super Bowl games through January 1994. Note that since the Super Bowl is always played in January, the date of the game does not reflect the season just completed. Super Bowl I was played in January 1967 but was the climax of the 1966 season.

Super Bowl I

Played: January 15, 1967, at the Memorial Coliseum in Los Angeles, California.
Attendance: 61,946.
Final score: Green Bay Packers 35, Kansas City Chiefs 10.

The Packers dominated the game with Bart Starr's passing and a tight defense. A 21-0 second half put the game out of Kansas City's reach. Starr threw for 250 yards, veteran receiver Max McGee caught seven passes for 138 yards, and safety Willie Wood lugged an interception back 50 yards to ensure the Pack and the NFL a big victory.

Super Bowl II

Played: January 14, 1968, at the Orange Bowl in Miami, Florida.
Attendance: 75,546.
Final score: Green Bay Packers 33, Oakland Raiders 14.

The Packers used the same formula for a second straight year. Starr was a third-down wonder. Boyd Dowler caught a 62-yard TD toss and Herb Adderley ran an interception back 60 yards for a score. Three field goals by Don Chandler also helped make Vince Lombardi's final game as the Packer coach a memorable one.

Super Bowl III

Played: January 12, 1969, at the Orange Bowl in Miami, Florida.
Attendance: 75,389.
Final score: New York Jets 16, Baltimore Colts 7.

One of the great upsets in sports history and the first Super Bowl win for an AFL team. This was the game in which the brash young Jets quarterback Joe Namath "guaranteed" a victory, infuriating the Colts, a team that had finished in the regular season with a 13-1 record. But Namath threw for 206 yards, fullback Matt Snell ran for 121, and the Jets' big offensive line neutralized the Colts' great defense. The game not only put the AFL on the map, but made pro football bigger than ever.

Super Bowl IV

Played: January 11, 1970, at Tulane Stadium in New Orleans, Louisiana.
Attendance: 80,562.
Final score: Kansas City Chiefs 23, Minnesota Vikings 7.

Another upset. The underdog Chiefs used a balanced offense and a great defense to dominate the powerful Vikings. Quarterback Len Dawson completed 12 of 17, including an exciting 46-yard pass/run touchdown play to receiver Otis Taylor. The Chiefs dominated the line of scrimmage and intercepted the Viking quarterbacks three times. Super Bowl IV was the final game before the National and American Football Leagues merged. From this point on it was all one big National Football League, with the old AFL teams and three NFL clubs forming the American Conference. The other NFL clubs were in the National Conference. The conference winners would play in the future Super Bowls.

Super Bowl V

Played: January 17, 1971, at the Orange Bowl in Miami, Florida.

Attendance: 79,204.

Final score: Baltimore Colts 16, Dallas Cowboys 13.

Often called the "Blooper Bowl," this was an error-filled contest that was exciting only because it went down to the final seconds. Six passes were intercepted, with Dallas linebacker Chuck Howley getting a pair and the MVP prize. Baltimore scored a fourth-quarter touchdown to tie it, then left it up to a little-known placekicker named Jim O'Brien to boot a 32-yard field goal in the final five seconds to win football's biggest prize.

Super Bowl VI

Played: January 16, 1972, at Tulane Stadium in New Orleans, Louisiana.

Attendance: 81,023.

Final score: Dallas Cowboys 24, Miami Dolphins 3.

After losing a close one the year before, the Cowboys took no chances against the Dolphins. They won it with a steady offense that produced points in each period and a dominating defense that stopped the vaunted Miami running game. Duane Thomas ran for 95 yards, Walt Garrison for 74, and the cool, accurate Roger Staubach completed 12 of 19 passes for two scores to highlight the Dallas win. An expansion team in 1960, the Cowboys had become a top team in less than a decade and seemed determined to stay there.

Super Bowl VII

Played: January 14, 1973, at the Memorial Coliseum in Los Angeles, California.
Attendance: 90,182.
Final score: Miami Dolphins 14, Washington Redskins 7.

This was the game that completed the Dolphins' record-breaking unbeaten season. Coach George Allen's Redskins were a tough opponent but couldn't overcome a 14-0 Miami halftime lead. The Dolphins controlled the ball, with Larry Csonka running for 112 yards. Quarterback Bob Griese had to throw just 11 passes, but completed eight of them. Washington's only score came when Miami kicker Garo Yepremian tried to pass after a bad snap and fumbled the ball to Washington's Mike Bass, who ran it back 49 yards for the TD.

Super Bowl VIII

Played: January 13, 1974, at Rice Stadium in Houston, Texas.
Attendance: 71,882.
Final score: Miami Dolphins 24, Minnesota Vikings 7.

The Dolphins made it two straight with a convincing victory over the Vikings. It was 17-0 at the half and 24-0 after three before Fran Tarkenton and the Vikings could get on the scoreboard. Griese again let his runners do the work as he completed six of just seven passes for 73 yards. But Larry Csonka ran for 145 yards on 33 carries, then a Super Bowl record, and the Dolphins' so-called "No-Name Defense" did a superb job for a second straight season.

Super Bowl IX

Played: January 12, 1975, at Tulane Stadium in New Orleans, Louisiana.
Attendance: 80,997.
Final score: Pittsburgh Steelers 16, Minnesota Vikings 6.

It was the start of the Steeler dynasty and a continuation of the Vikings' frustration. Pittsburgh had never won a title of any kind since coming into the league in 1933. But a team with the likes of Terry Bradshaw, Franco Harris, Lynn Swann, John Stallworth, Mean Joe Greene, Jack Ham, Jack Lambert, and Mel Blount had talent to burn. Harris set a Super Bowl rushing mark with 158 yards, and the defense intercepted three Fran Tarkenton passes to highlight the victory. And the Steelers were far from finished.

Super Bowl X

Played: January 18, 1976, at the Orange Bowl in Miami, Florida.
Attendance: 80,187.
Final score: Pittsburgh Steelers 21, Dallas Cowboys 17.

A great rivalry between two powerhouse teams. Both were explosive on offense, big and tough on defense. The difference in this one was receiver Lynn Swann. The acrobatic pass-catcher made several absolutely brilliant grabs, catching four Bradshaw passes for 161 yards and a 64-yard touchdown. Two fourth-quarter Steeler touchdowns erased a 10-7 Dallas lead, and the Pittsburgh defense sacked the usually elusive Roger Staubach seven times in a classic battle.

Super Bowl XI

Played: January 9, 1977, at the Rose Bowl in Pasadena, California.

Attendance: 103,438.

Final score: Oakland Raiders 32, Minnesota Vikings 14.

Almost more attention was paid to the Vikings' fourth Super Bowl loss than the Raiders' victory. But Coach John Madden's team was a fine one, led by quarterback Ken "the Snake" Stabler and a rock-solid defense. Stabler threw for 180 yards while halfback Clarence Davis ran for 137. But it was a real team effort, helped by veteran defensive back Willie Brown's 75-yard touchdown run after he intercepted a Fran Tarkenton pass. "The Raiders completely dominated us," Tarkenton admitted.

Super Bowl XII

Played: January 15, 1978, at the Louisiana Superdome in New Orleans, Louisiana.

Attendance: 75,583.

Final score: Dallas Cowboys 27, Denver Broncos 10.

Tom Landry's Cowboys were back again, in a game dominated by their "doomsday" defense. The defense held the Bronco quarterbacks to just eight completions in 25 tries for 61 yards. And when the passes weren't incomplete, they were being picked off. Dallas stole four tosses. Meanwhile, Roger Staubach was throwing for 183 yards, including a 45-yard touchdown toss to Butch Johnson. The combination gave the Cowboys another championship.

Super Bowl XIII

Played: January 21, 1979,
at the Orange Bowl in Miami,
Florida.
Attendance: 79,484.
Final score: Pittsburgh Steelers
35, Dallas Cowboys 31.

One of the most competitive
Super Bowls ever. The two old
rivals battled tooth and nail right
up to the final gun. Even the stats
were almost a standoff.
Dallas gained more on the
ground; Pittsburgh more through the
air. Terry Bradshaw threw for 318 yards
and four scores, John Stallworth catching two of them, including a dramatic
75-yarder. Roger Staubach tossed into
the end zone three times, including a
pair in the fourth quarter that made it
close. The Jolly Roger was always one
of the great comeback quarterbacks in
football, but the Steelers prevailed for a
third Super Bowl crown.

Super Bowl XIV

Played: January 20, 1980, at the
Rose Bowl in Pasadena, California.
Attendance: 103,985.
Final score: Pittsburgh Steelers 31,
Los Angeles Rams 19.

This was a hard-fought battle that marked
the crowning achievement of the Pittsburgh
dynasty of the 1970s. More than ever, the
Steelers had to ride home on the strong arm
of quarterback Terry Bradshaw. Despite Bradshaw's outstanding play,
the Rams held a 19-17 lead after three quarters. But a 73-yard scoring
pass to John Stallworth gave the Steelers the lead for good. A clutch
drive later in the fourth quarter, highlighted by a 45-yard pass to
Stallworth, gave the Steelers seven insurance points. Bradshaw threw

for 309 yards, while Stallworth caught three for 121 yards to highlight the victory that made Pittsburgh the first team to win the Super Bowl four times.

Super Bowl XV

Played: January 25, 1981, at the Louisiana Superdome in New Orleans, Louisiana.
Attendance: 76,135.
Final score: Oakland Raiders 27, Philadelphia Eagles 10.

Many thought this one would be a lot closer, but the Raiders came through in fine style behind quarterback Jim Plunkett, considered washed up a short time before. Plunkett struck early, throwing for a pair of scores in the first quarter and another in the third. Mark van Eeghen ran for 80 yards on 19 carries to balance the attack while the Raider defense, spearheaded by linebacker Rod Martin's three interceptions, put a halt to the Eagles' offense.

Super Bowl XVI

Played: January 24, 1982, at the Pontiac Silverdome in Pontiac, Michigan.
Attendance: 81,270.
Final score: San Francisco 49ers 26, Cincinnati Bengals 21.

A new king was about to be crowned. The Niners had rebuilt under Coach Bill Walsh and quarterback Joe Montana. In their Super Bowl debut they took a 20-0 halftime lead over the Bengals, then had to withstand a furious Cincy rally to win it. In the Bengals' final touchdown drive quarterback Ken Anderson completed six straight passes en route to a 300-yard game. The Bengals actually outgained the Niners by 81 yards.

Super Bowl XVII

Played: January 30, 1983, at the Rose Bowl in Pasadena, California.

Attendance: 103,667.

Final score: Washington Redskins 27, Miami Dolphins 17.

Hail to the Redskins. Washington overcame a 17-10 halftime deficit behind the play of quarterback Joe Theismann and veteran fullback John Riggins to win its first Super Bowl. Riggins's 43-yard scoring run early in the fourth quarter gave the Skins the lead, and Theismann put it away with a six-yard TD toss to Charlie Brown later in the period. Riggins slammed around and through the vaunted Miami defense for a Super Bowl record 166 yards on 38 carries. He controlled the ball, the clock, and eventually the game.

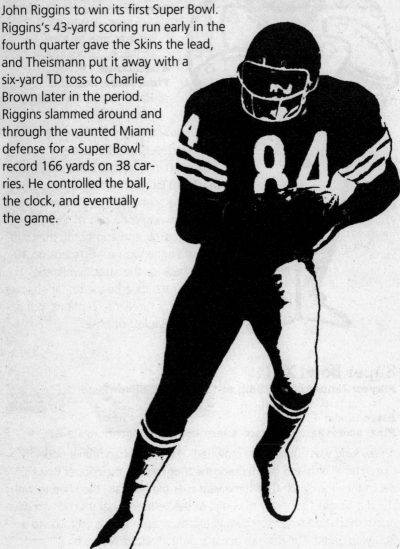

Super Bowl XVIII

Played: January 22, 1984, at Tampa Stadium in Tampa, Florida.
Attendance: 72,920.
Final score: Los Angeles Raiders 38, Washington Redskins 9.

This turned out to be the most lopsided Super Bowl win to date. The Raiders did it against a Washington club that was 14-2 in the regular season and considered the classiest team in the league. L.A. took over early with veteran quarterback Jim Plunkett and halfback Marcus Allen leading the way. It was a 21-3 game at the half and the Skins never really challenged. In the third quarter, Allen made perhaps the most electrifying broken-field run in Super Bowl history, scampering 74-yards for a touchdown. He wound up breaking John Riggins's one-year-old Super Bowl rushing record with 191 yards on just 20 carries in an MVP performance.

Super Bowl XIX

Played: January 20, 1985, at Stanford Stadium in Palo Alto, California.
Attendance: 84,059.
Final score: San Francisco 49ers 38, Miami Dolphins 16.

This was expected to be a shootout between Joe Montana and the Dolphins' young, record-breaking quarterback Dan Marino. But the 49ers were on the brink of being crowned the team of the 1980s and weren't about to lose this one. In fact, the game turned pretty much into a blowout. Montana was brilliant; he completed 24 of 35 passes, good for a record 331 yards and three scores. In addition, the Niners ran for 211 yards to just 25 for the Dolphins. It was a total victory.

Miami Dolphins quarterback Dan Marino

Super Bowl XX

Played: January 26, 1986, at the Louisiana Superdome in New Orleans, Louisiana.

Attendance: 73,818.

Final score: Chicago Bears 46, New England Patriots 10.

Regaining some of their glory from an earlier time, the Chicago Bears took their first title since 1963 and did it the old-fashioned way, completely overpowering the Patriots. A fumble recovery of the opening kickoff led to a quick New England field goal. After that, it was all Bears. They sacked Pats quarterbacks seven times and held New England to a record-low seven yards rushing. Meanwhile, Chicago quarterback Jim McMahon, halfback Walter Payton, and wide receiver Willie Gault led an offensive blast that took care of business very efficiently.

Super Bowl XXI

Played: January 25, 1987, at the Rose Bowl in Pasadena, California.

Attendance: 101,063.

Final score: New York Giants 39, Denver Broncos 20.

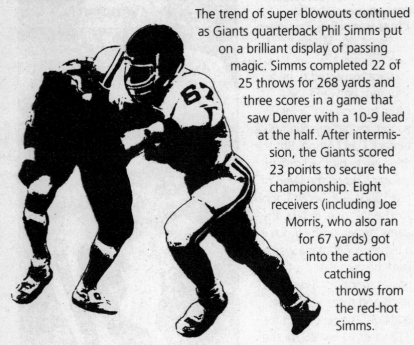

The trend of super blowouts continued as Giants quarterback Phil Simms put on a brilliant display of passing magic. Simms completed 22 of 25 throws for 268 yards and three scores in a game that saw Denver with a 10-9 lead at the half. After intermission, the Giants scored 23 points to secure the championship. Eight receivers (including Joe Morris, who also ran for 67 yards) got into the action catching throws from the red-hot Simms.

Super Bowl XXII

Played: January 31, 1988, at San Diego Jack Murphy Stadium in San Diego, California.
Attendance: 73,302.
Final score: Washington Redskins 42, Denver Broncos 10.

The Broncos went down to their third Super Bowl defeat in three tries. This time Denver took a 10-0 lead in the first quarter before being left in the dust by Washington's amazing offensive display. With quarterback Doug Williams throwing four touchdown passes in the second quarter alone, the Redskins scored 35 unanswered points to blow the game open. Williams threw for 228 of his 340 passing yards in the second quarter. He was 18 for 29 on the day and got tremendous support from rookie fullback Timmy Smith, who set a Super Bowl mark with 204 rushing yards on 22 carries.

Super Bowl XXIII

Played: January 22, 1989, at Joe Robbie Stadium in Miami, Florida.
Attendance: 75,129.
Final score: San Francisco 49ers 20, Cincinnati Bengals 16.

A rematch of Super Bowl XVI and another very close game. This time the Niners had to come from behind in the fourth quarter, but that's always been a specialty of Joe Montana's. Known as "the comeback kid" since his Notre Dame days, Montana tossed a pair of final-session TDs, one to All-World receiver Jerry Rice and the other to John Taylor for the victory. The final drive covered 92 yards with the winning pass coming from the 10-yard line with just 34 seconds remaining. Rice had 11 catches for a Super Bowl mark of 215 yards and an MVP trophy.

San Francisco 49ers quarterback Joe Montana

Super Bowl XXIV

Played: January 28, 1990, at the Louisiana Superdome in New Orleans, Louisiana.
Attendance: 72,919.
Final score: San Francisco 49ers 55, Denver Broncos 10.

What can you say about a Super Bowl game with a 55-10 final score. The Broncos again. But remember, it takes an outstanding team just to reach the Super Bowl. The Niners were a dynasty at the top of their game, winning the big one for a fourth time. Montana and company were virtually unstoppable. Super Joe completed 22 of 29 passes for 297 yards and a record five touchdowns. Jerry Rice caught seven for 148 yards and three scores. The Niners were so consistent that after scoring 13 points in the first quarter they scored 14 in each of the next three.

Super Bowl XXV

Played: January 27, 1991, at Tampa Stadium in Tampa, Florida.
Attendance: 73,813.
Final score: New York Giants 20, Buffalo Bills 19.

A beauty from start to finish, one of the most competitive Super Bowls ever and decided by a margin of only one foot. It was tied at 3-3 after the first quarter. The Bills led 12-10 at the half, the Giants 17-12 after session three. Buffalo came back for a 19-17 lead only to have the Giants drive downfield once again, taking 14 plays before Matt Bahr booted a 21-yard field goal to make it a 20-19 game. With 2:16 left, Buffalo moved again. There were eight seconds left when the Bills' Scott Norwood set up for the possible winning 47-yard field goal. The ball was up, long enough, and … just wide to the right by about a foot. Wow. This was a game to remember.

Super Bowl XXVI

Played: January 26, 1992, at the Hubert H. Humphrey Metrodome in Minneapolis, Minnesota.
Attendance: 63,130.
Final score: Washington Redskins 37, Buffalo Bills 24.

The Bills were back again, only this time facing a Redskins team that had fire in its eyes. The fire flared after a scoreless first period. Led by quarterback Mark Rypien, the Skins scored 17 points before halftime, then cruised to victory. Rypien threw for 292 yards and a pair of scores. When the Skins intercepted Jim Kelly's first pass of the second half and turned it into a score, it broke the backs of the Bills. Kelly set a Super Bowl record by throwing 58 passes in a come-from-behind effort that fell short.

Super Bowl XXVII

Played: January 31, 1993, at the Rose Bowl in Pasadena, California.
Attendance: 98,374.
Final score: Dallas Cowboys 52, Buffalo Bills 17.

There were a lot of stories here. The Cowboys had rebuilt from a 1-15 season just three years earlier under coach Jimmy Johnson. The Bills were trying to avoid the embarrassing record of being the first team to lose three straight Super Bowls. Buffalo scored first after a blocked punt, but then the roof fell in. No one expected the kind of onslaught that followed. Dallas quarterback Troy Aikman threw for 148 yards and three scores before halftime. He would end up with a 22 of 30 day for 273 yards and four scores. After the game, Aikman said something that could have been said by Bart Starr or Joe Namath or another star quarterback since January 1967: "Someday I can look back and say I took a team to the Super Bowl and won it." It's the ultimate.

Super Bowl XXVIII

Played: January 30, 1994, at the Georgia Dome in Atlanta, Georgia.
Attendance: 72,817.
Final score: Dallas Cowboys 30, Buffalo Bills 13.

For the first 30 minutes it looked as if the Bills would break their 0-for-3 Super Bowl hex. With Jim Kelly running the offense smoothly and conservatively, and the Bruce Smith-led defense stopping the vaunted Dallas attack, Buffalo took a 13-6 lead into the halftime locker room. But a 46-yard James Washington touchdown return of a Thurman Thomas fumble in the first minute of the second half turned things around. After that, it went according to script. Emmitt Smith produced an MVP performance with 132 yards on 30 carries, and the Cowboys won going away. It was their second straight Super victory, and more people began talking of a dynasty in the nineties.

Super Bowl
Most Valuable Players

Super Bowl I ....Quarterback Bart Starr,
Green Bay

Super Bowl II..............Quarterback Bart Starr,
Green Bay

Super Bowl III ....Quarterback Joe Namath,
New York Jets

Super Bowl IV ....Quarterback Len Dawson,
Kansas City

Super Bowl V ....Linebacker Chuck Howley
Dallas

Super Bowl VI ....Quarterback Roger Staubach,
Dallas

Super Bowl VII..................Safety Jake Scott,
Miami

Super Bowl VIII.......Running back Larry Csonka,
Miami

Super Bowl IX ....Running back Franco Harris,
Pittsburgh

Super Bowl X ....Wide receiver Lynn Swann,
Pittsburgh

Super Bowl XI ......Wide receiver Fred Biletnikoff,
Oakland

Super Bowl XII ..Defensive tackle Randy White and
defensive end Harvey Martin,
Dallas (co-winners)

Super Bowl
Most Valuable Players
(continued)

Super Bowl XIII ..... Quarterback Terry Bradshaw, Pittsburgh

Super Bowl XIV ..... Quarterback Terry Bradshaw, Pittsburgh

Super Bowl XV .... Quarterback Jim Plunkett, Oakland

Super Bowl XVI .... Quarterback Joe Montana, San Francisco

Super Bowl XVII ...... Running back John Riggins, Washington

Super Bowl XVIII ..... Running back Marcus Allen, L.A. Raiders

Super Bowl XIX .... Quarterback Joe Montana, San Francisco

Super Bowl XX .... Defensive end Richard Dent, Chicago

Super Bowl XXI .... Quarterback Phil Simms, New York Giants

Super Bowl XXII .... Quarterback Doug Williams, Washington

Super Bowl XXIII .... Wide receiver Jerry Rice, San Francisco

Super Bowl XXIV .... Quarterback Joe Montana, San Francisco

Super Bowl
Most Valuable Players

(continued)

Super Bowl XXV.....Running back Ottis Anderson,
New York Giants

Super Bowl XXVI.......Quarterback Mark Rypien,
Washington

Super Bowl XXVII......Quarterback Troy Aikman,
Dallas

Super Bowl XXVIII...Running back Emmitt Smith,
Dallas

Emmitt Smith

8

Some Strange and Unexpected Moments in NFL History

They happen in every sport, those unusual moments that seem to come out of nowhere, sometimes in the heat of battle, other times before or after the game. You might find yourself looking twice just to make sure your eyes weren't playing tricks on you. Strange and unexpected moments on the gridiron have happened from the beginning. Here are some of the better ones.

OUT FROM THE COLD

Indoor football is as common as cable television these days. Huge, domed indoor stadiums have been built in many American cities, especially those with extreme temperatures, hot or cold. But in the early days, football was strictly an outdoor game. No matter what the weather.

In 1932, the Chicago Bears and Portsmouth Spartans finished the regular season in a tie and had to play one game for the NFL title. The game was set for Wrigley Field, but when the weather turned brutal with ice, cold, and snow the game was moved to Chicago Stadium. There was one catch: Chicago Stadium was an indoor arena.

The game resembled arena football of today. The field was just 80 yards long, rounded at the corners because of the boards around the arena. When a play ended near the sidelines the ball was brought close to the middle of the field so that players wouldn't crash into the boards. Fortunately, the circus had been in town and the floor was covered with dirt. Otherwise, the game would have been played on concrete. Now that would have been really amazing. P.S.: The Bears won, 9-0.

THREE KOs FOR NAGURSKI

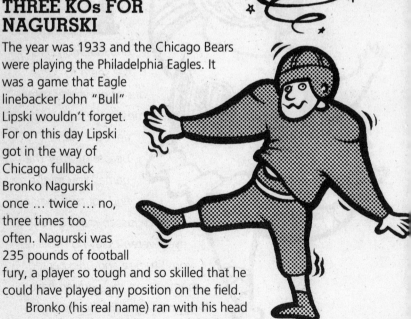

The year was 1933 and the Chicago Bears were playing the Philadelphia Eagles. It was a game that Eagle linebacker John "Bull" Lipski wouldn't forget. For on this day Lipski got in the way of Chicago fullback Bronko Nagurski once … twice … no, three times too often. Nagurski was 235 pounds of football fury, a player so tough and so skilled that he could have played any position on the field.

Bronko (his real name) ran with his head down, his body low to the ground, his knees pumping high. He was tough to tackle and punished opponents on every play. He was also able to block two, three, or sometimes more men on a single play.

Early in the game Nagurski had the football and Lipski tried to tackle him. The two had a head-on collision. When the smoke cleared, Nagurski was still running and Lipski was out cold. He was helped from the field, but minutes later he was back in the game. Sure enough, Nagurski carried again and once again Lipski hit him. Bingo. Lipski was out cold a second time.

As the next play started Nagurski carried on the sweep. Two Eagle subs were still helping the dizzy Lipski to the sidelines. BAM. Nagurski plowed into all three of them and Bull Lipski was knocked out a third time, making him perhaps the only player in NFL history to be knocked cold three times in the same game—by the same player.

TURNABOUT IS FAIR PLAY

Any athlete is going to have good days and bad days. But what happened to Jim Hardy during an eight-day span in 1950 was ridiculous. Hardy was the quarterback of the Chicago Cardinals and on September 24 led his team against the Philadelphia Eagles in the season opener.

Suddenly, everything began going wrong. Jim Hardy was having one of those nightmare days quarterbacks dread. Before it ended, he had thrown a record eight interceptions. The Eagles' Russ Craft picked off four and Joe Sutton three. Hardy also fumbled three times and completed just 12 of 39 passes. The Cardinals lost, 45-7.

On October 2 the Cards returned to the field against the Colts. Hardy was at quarterback again, probably fearful of losing his job with a repeat of the opener. Instead, he was on fire, connecting all over the field. In the space of a week, Jim Hardy went from throwing eight interceptions to firing six touchdown passes. Receiver Bob Shaw set a record by catching five of them as the Cardinals won, 55-13.

HEY JIM, THIS WAY

Jim Marshall of the Minnesota Vikings was one of the finer defensive ends of his time, a Pro Bowler who never missed a game. But that didn't mean he didn't occasionally lose his bearings. What he did on October 25, 1964, in a game against the 49ers will go down as part of football's wacky legend.

With the Vikings leading, 27-17, in the fourth quarter, the powerful Minnesota defense caused a fumble. Several players went for the ball but Marshall got there first. He scooped it up and started running as the players, coaches, and fans erupted in screams and yells. They had good reason to yell.

Jim Marshall was running the WRONG WAY!

As he crossed the San Francisco goal line he saw Vikes quarterback Fran Tarkenton on the sidelines pointing the other way. In desperation, Marshall threw the ball in the direction of Tarkenton. It rolled out of bounds and was ruled a safety, two points for the Niners.

Fortunately, the Vikings held on to win, but Marshall's 60-yard, wrong-way jaunt made all the highlight films and was really one for the books.

OORANG ON THE WARPATH

No one will dispute the talent of Jim Thorpe. He was simply one of the greatest football players ever. But by the time the American Professional Football Association (which soon became the NFL) was formed in 1920, Thorpe was 32 years old and beginning to slow down. He joined the Canton Bulldogs but two years later became restless. What followed was a very strange episode.

Thorpe, who was part Sac-Fox Indian, decided to put together a team of Indian players, the only time in NFL history that a team was intended to follow strict ethnic and racial lines. Fortunately, there were several outstanding Indian players around, men like Joe Guyon and Pete Calas. But then the Indian talent thinned.

So Thorpe was forced to bring in some ringers, players who weren't really Indians. The team was named the Oorang Indians. But "Oorang" wasn't even an Indian name. It was the name of a local dog kennel that sponsored the team. Oorang played out of Marion, Ohio, and wasn't very good. The team was 2-6 in 1922 and a woeful 1-10 in 1923. In one game in which Thorpe didn't play, Oorang was beaten by Akron, 66-0. After 1923 they were gone.

While they competed the Oorang players were called Running Deer, Gray Horse, Eagle Feather, Tomahawk, Little Twig, and other names that made them sound like Indians. Imagine if someone tried to do that today!

MAGIC SHOES

In December 1934 the New York Giants and Chicago Bears got ready to battle it out for the NFL championship. The game was played in the old Polo Grounds in New York, and the weather was downright mean—frigid and windy—and the field frozen solid.

Footing was uncertain. The players' cleats weren't even biting into the hard turf. Still, the powerful Bears took a 10-3 lead into the locker room at halftime. That's when New York coach Steve Owen decided to take the advice of one of his players, Ray Flaherty, who had said that basketball shoes gave better traction on a hard field than cleats.

Owen called a friend at Manhattan College who said he would send a batch of sneakers to the Polo Grounds (the Giants' home stadium back then). But when the third quarter started, the sneakers weren't there, and the Bears upped their lead to 13-3. Then the clubhouse man appeared with an armload of sneakers, with more stuffed in his pockets and under his coat.

The New York Giants players simply dove into the pile and searched for their sizes. Within minutes, all the players were wearing sneakers. When they returned to the field, it was as if magic had taken place. The Giants began flying, gaining ground on long passes and long runs. They scored, and scored again and again.

When it ended, the magic sneakers had led to 27 fourth-quarter points and a 30-13 New York victory, perhaps the only time an NFL championship was won by a heroic clubhouse man with an armload of sneakers.

HEIDI ANYONE?

Johanna Spyri's book *Heidi* is one of the most beloved children's stories ever told. The heartwarming tale of the little girl and her grandfather in the Swiss Alps has been read by youngsters for more than a century, and watched in several movie and television versions. But what happens when *Heidi* is suddenly sprung on a million hard-nosed football fans watching a great game?

It happened on November 17, 1968. The Oakland Raiders and New York Jets were in the middle of a heated game televised nationally by NBC. At the end of three periods the Raiders had a 22-19 lead, but Jets quarterback Joe Namath hit Don Maynard with a 50-yard TD strike to put the New Yorkers in front. Oakland returned the favor and had a 29-26 lead before the Jets' Jim Turner kicked a pair of late field goals to put New York back in front, 32-29, with just over a minute left. The second field goal occurred at exactly 7 P.M. on the East Coast, and suddenly the game was gone as NBC switched to the credits for the beginning of a new movie version of *Heidi*.

Football fans didn't know what to think. Although the Jets had a three-point lead, who knew what the Raiders would do in the final minute. The Jets would probably win, but …

As Heidi's story began to unfold, another drama was taking place in Oakland. The Raiders' Daryle Lamonica threw a 43-yard touchdown

pass to Charlie Smith to give his team a 36-32 lead. And when the Jets fumbled the ensuing kickoff, Oakland's Preston Ridlehuber scooped it up and ran it into the end zone for yet another score. The last-minute lightning gave the Raiders a 43-32 victory.

When East Coast fans found out, they went berserk. Network switchboards were jammed with complaining phone calls. Fans called the newspapers, other TV stations, and even the police. Some callers didn't know the outcome of the game, and when they found out, they became even more enraged. The network was forced to issue a public apology. After that, all NFL games were allowed to run to conclusion.

But one has to wonder how many of those irate football fans, missing the exciting end of a great game, took their wrath out on poor Heidi and never allowed their children to mention that endearing girl again.

WHAT'S A GREEN BAY PACKER?

Ever wonder how a team gets its nickname? A variety of ways, of course. Bears, Giants, Eagles, Jets, Raiders, Rams, Cowboys. It's easy to understand why they are nicknames of pro football teams. But the Packers, that old and respected franchise. What is a Green Bay Packer?

Actually, it's a rather unusual story. The prime mover in the formation of the franchise was Earl "Curly" Lambeau. Lambeau was born and raised in Green Bay, then went to college at Notre Dame, where he was one of the football team's star players. In 1919 he was back home taking a job with the Indian Packing Company of Green Bay. The company packed processed meats.

A short time later Curly Lambeau decided he wanted to start a professional football team. He went to the president of the company and asked for $500 to buy jerseys, pads, footballs, and pants. In return, he promised that the team would be called the Packers.

Two years later the Packers were in the newly organized professional football league, and when the Indian Packing Company was purchased shortly afterward, Lambeau borrowed money and bought the team himself. By 1923 the club was a community-owned, nonprofit corporation, and has remained in Green Bay ever since.

The team has also stayed the "Packers," the only football team named after a meat-packing company. Maybe that's what Vince Lombardi's Packers did, too. They pretty much packed all their opponents away in the 1960s.

A 1,000-YARD RUNNER, OR IS HE?

Dave Hampton could never crack the starting lineup at Green Bay. The speedy halfback gained a total of 787 yards in three seasons with the Packers before being traded to the Atlanta Falcons prior to the 1972 season. As the featured back with the Falcons, Hampton set his sights on that annual goal for all outstanding runners—1,000 yards.

Sure enough, given a chance to play regularly Hampton proved he was indeed one of the better running backs in the NFL. On December 17, the Falcons were playing their final regular-season game and Dave Hampton had 930 yards. He needed 70 more to hit 1,000.

In the fourth period, Hampton carried for his 70th yard of the day, giving him an even 1,000. The game was stopped and Hampton was given the ball. But it wasn't over yet. Hampton had to go back to work. On his next carry, he was nailed for a six-yard loss. That meant his total gain was again under 1,000 yards. It couldn't be happening. With the clock running down fast, Hampton got just one more carry and gained a mere yard. So after all the pomp and ceremony, not to mention the game ball, Dave Hampton was credited with 995 yards on the year.

But that isn't the end of the story. A year later Hampton was back and running well again. This time he came into the final game with 913 yards, 87 short of 1,000. Once again Hampton gave it all he had, carrying the ball 27 times. But he could gain only 84 yards, bringing his total to 997. He was just short again.

Persistence, however, finally paid off. After running for only 464 yards in 1974, Hampton was back in top form in 1975. Of course, he went into the final game short of his goal, needing 59 yards to reach 1,000. This time he made it, but not by much. He ran for 61 yards to finish at 1,002 for the season.

Falcon fans always had to look very closely to see if Dave Hampton made his 1,000 yards, sometimes waiting until his final carry of the year.

LEASE A QUARTERBACK

No, this is not a football version of Hertz or Avis. You're not supposed to rent or lease athletes, at least not in pro football. But before the 1964 season started in the old American Football League, the Denver Broncos and Houston Oilers completed a strange transaction.

The Broncos were coming off a 2-11-1 season and badly needed a quarterback. They approached the Oilers inquiring about Jacky Lee, a youngster who was George Blanda's backup but was thought to have potential. The resultant deal was one of the strangest in pro sports.

The Oilers received defensive lineman Bud McFadin, a first-round draft choice, and cash for the services of Jacky Lee. Seemed fair enough. But the Broncos were getting Lee for only two seasons; in effect, they were leasing him. After two years, he would return to Houston or another agreement would have to be reached.

Lee played two years in Denver and performed fairly well for a poor team. But no new deal was made. After two seasons Lee was sent back to Houston, marking perhaps the only time in pro football history that a quarterback was leased and then returned.

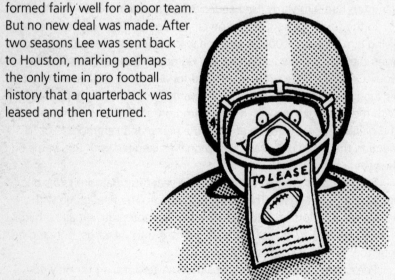

ROCKNE CHALLENGES THE PROS

One of the strangest football games ever took place in 1930, when college football still reigned supreme over the pro game in the eyes of many fans. Knute Rockne, the already legendary coach of Notre Dame, thought so little of professional football that he said he could put together an All-Star team of former collegians that would beat any pro team.

Finally, a game was set up. It would be a benefit for the unemployed and would feature a Rockne All-Star team against the New York Giants. The Giants were led by quarterback and coach Benny Friedman, a highly intelligent and talented player who loved a challenge. Bring on Rockne, he said.

Rockne figured his team would be more motivated, not to mention quicker, than the pros. He told them to score a couple of touchdowns early, then hold the Giants at bay. Easier said than done. The Giants came out with fire in their eyes and pushed the former college standouts all over the field.

Friedman was the star. At one point he ran 25 yards for a score, toppling several opponents on the way. He scored 13 of the Giants' 22 points in a 22-0 whitewash. Observers said it could have been 70-0 if Friedman hadn't finally shown some mercy.

As for Rockne's collegians, their net yardage on the day was a minus-30. Perhaps it was this strange game that showed once and for all that the pros were the best football players in the world.

KILMER'S AMAZING COMEBACK

In 1962 Billy Kilmer was a promising second-year quarterback for the San Francisco 49ers. Kilmer had been an All-American tailback at UCLA. He wasn't a great thrower, but the Niners were putting in a shotgun formation and wanted a quarterback who could run and throw.

One day after practice Kilmer began driving back to the city. He either fell asleep at the wheel or was cut off. He couldn't remember, not after his car careened some 435 feet down a steep embankment and through a field, coming to rest in a ditch. Kilmer's right leg was badly fractured. By the time rescuers reached him, the muddy water in the ditch had begun to infect the leg.

At first the doctors feared the leg would have to come off. Then they told Kilmer he would never walk normally again. They also told him football was out. Period. But they didn't know about the grit and determination of Billy Kilmer. He sat out the 1963 season, but all he thought about was coming back.

"I figured I was just too young to give it up," he said.

By 1964 Kilmer was back in the Niners' training camp. He actually tried to convert to running back for a while. Then, in 1967, he was traded to New Orleans where he became a fine quarterback. His best days came after 1971, when he went to the Washington Redskins. Playing until he was nearly 40, Kilmer was a leader and a winner, if never a picture passer. He was one of the most colorful quarterbacks ever, something no one thought possible after he was dragged from his wrecked car in 1962.

9

NFL **Trivia**
Takes

There are so many little
things that have happened
in the NFL over the years;
so many firsts and lasts, milestones,
and unusual incidents that it's
impossible to list them all. Here is a
rundown of a few bits of NFL trivia.
For further details you can always
look 'em up.

Mike Reid

An All-American defensive tackle at Penn State who went on to become an All-Pro defensive tackle with the Cincinnati Bengals, Mike Reid retired from football in 1974 at age 27. That's because he wanted a career in music and is probably the only all-pro defensive tackle to become a Grammy-winning songwriter. He is also a top country music performer.

Michael Carter

In the space of five months, Michael Carter went from being a silver medalist in the shot put at the 1984 Olympic Games to being a reserve lineman with the San Francisco 49ers in the season that they won Super Bowl XIX.

Lyle Alzado

One of the real tough guys in the NFL, Lyle Alzado, who died in 1992, was never one to back away from a challenge. In 1979, the defensive tackle fought an eight-round boxing exhibition in Denver against retired heavyweight champion Muhammad Ali—and Alzado finished on his feet.

Lionel Taylor

He was the first player in either the American Football League or National Football League to catch 100 passes in a season. Taylor grabbed an even 100 for the Denver Broncos of the AFL in 1961.

R. C. Owens

This former San Francisco 49er is the man who started the "Alley Oop" play in 1957, his rookie year. Owens, a 6'3" wide receiver who could jump, suggested that quarterback Y. A. Tittle throw high and hit him at the top of his leap. They became one of the most colorful passing combos of the 1950s.

Don Hutson

The famed "Alabama Antelope" was the first wide receiver to gain more than 1,000 yards receiving for a season. Receiving stats were kept beginning in 1932, but it wasn't until 1942 that Hutson broke the 1,000-yard barrier by catching 74 passes for 1,211 yards and 17 touchdowns for the Green Bay Packers.

Fred Gehrke

A halfback with the Los Angeles Rams in 1948, Fred Gehrke changed the look of pro football. He took the plain leather helmets the team wore, painted them blue, and then added a ram's horn to each side. That started the trend to team emblems on helmets. The Rams still use the horn emblem today.

Carl Weathers

Weathers was a second-string linebacker with the Oakland Raiders in 1970 and 1971. His football career didn't last long, but his second career has. Weathers became an actor, and among his numerous roles is that of the fighter Apollo Creed in the first four Rocky films.

Sally Berry

Raymond Berry, a top Baltimore Colts receiver from 1955 to 1967, had a secret weapon on his route to All-Pro stardom: his wife Sally. Berry liked to practice so much that he often ran out of people to throw to him. Enter Sally. "She's got a good arm," Berry said. And he became one of the best ever.

Chuck Bednarik

This Philadelphia Eagles center/linebacker was the last of the two-way players. By 1960 the NFL featured platoon football, with separate offensive and defensive players. But when the Eagles met the Packers for the championship that year, the 35-year-old Bednarik played all 60 minutes and made the final tackle of the Pack's Jim Taylor to preserve a 17-13 Eagle victory.

Bill Osmanski

This fullback ran 68 yards for a touchdown on the second play of the 1940 championship game between the Chicago Bears and Washington Redskins. The TD opened the floodgates to Chicago's 73-0 victory, the most one-sided title game in NFL history.

Terry Bradshaw

The great Pittsburgh quarterback is best remembered for leading the Steelers to four Super Bowl titles. But Terry always had a super arm. As a high schooler in Shreveport, Louisiana, he set a then national prep-school record by throwing the javelin 243 feet, 7 inches.

Emlen Tunnell

Tunnell was the first black player elected to the Pro Football Hall of Fame. An outstanding defensive back with the New York Giants (11 years) and Green Bay Packers (3 years), Tunnell picked off 79 passes during his career, second on the all-time list.

Dan Devine

Devine had perhaps the roughest debut of any coach in NFL history. He became the Packers' head man in 1971 and in his team's first game, against the New York Giants, he got in the way as several players came flying across the sideline. Devine was carried from the field on a stretcher with a badly fractured leg.

Cliff Battles

On October 8, 1933, running back Battles had a big day for the old Boston Redskins when they met the New York Giants. He carried the ball just 16 times but wound up with an amazing 215 yards. What's more, he became the first runner in official NFL history to gain more than 200 yards in a game.

Alan Ameche

A big fullback and Heisman Trophy winner, Ameche made his pro debut for the Baltimore Colts against the Chicago Bears on September 25, 1955. On his very first NFL carry, the man who would become known as "the Horse" galloped for 79 yards and a touchdown. A great debut for a great player.

Joe Namath

"Broadway" Joe was a great quarterback and leader. But he did something else for pro football. When he came out of the University of Alabama, he signed a contract with the New York Jets for a then unheard of $400,000. It was part of the AFL-NFL price war and helped the leagues realize that in order to keep salaries from going too high they had to merge.

Bo Roberson

A sometimes explosive wide receiver with four AFL teams in the 1960s, Roberson also made his mark in another sport. He was the silver medalist in the long jump at the 1960 Olympics at Rome, runner-up to teammate Ralph Boston.

Bob Hayes

Another great Olympian-turned-football-player, Bob Hayes was known as the "world's fastest human" after winning the 100-meter dash at the 1964 Olympics in Tokyo. As a wide receiver with the Dallas Cowboys (ten years) and San Francisco 49ers (one year), the explosive Hayes grabbed 76 touchdown passes.

Richard Todd

The player who had the difficult task of following Joe Namath as New York Jets quarterback once did something that neither Broadway Joe nor any other NFL signal-caller could accomplish. In a game against the 49ers in 1980, Todd threw and threw and threw. When it ended, he had completed 42 passes, an NFL record. Wow.

Dave Winfield

One of the superstars of major league baseball, Winfield never played in the National Football League. But in the eyes of many he could have. Winny was such a great college athlete at Minnesota that he was drafted by the NFL Minnesota Vikings and the Atlanta Hawks of the National Basketball Association. But he chose baseball instead.

Doug Flutie

After one of the greatest college careers ever, quarterback Doug Flutie failed in short stints with several NFL teams. At 5'9" he was too small, they all said. So Flutie went north of the border to Calgary of the Canadian Football League and became the most exciting passer in Canada,

a record breaker. In Flutie's case, the NFL didn't know a good thing when it had it.

Ed Jones

"Too Tall" became an All-Pro defensive end with the Dallas Cowboys in the 1970s. But the 6'9" Jones felt restless and quit to pursue a boxing career in 1979. After just six bouts, however, Jones realized that the ring wars weren't for him, so he returned to the Cowboys and became an All-Pro once again.

Willie Thrower

Maybe the perfect name for a quarterback. But Thrower also made football history as the first black quarterback in the NFL. He played only one game, on October 18, 1953, completing three passes for the Chicago Bears in a contest against the 49ers. Not many people remember him, so it's a great trivia question.

Roger Staubach

Everyone knows what a great quarterback Roger Staubach was for the Dallas Cowboys. What they might not know is that Staubach was out of the game for five years while serving in the Navy after a great football career at Annapolis. He is the only service-academy player to become an All-Pro after sitting out for so long.

Roland Hooks

A little-known substitute half-back for the Buffalo Bills, Hooks played an almost perfect game against the Cincinnati Bengals on September 9, 1979. He carried the ball once in the first half, then returned in the second half to carry four more times. Each second-half carry, however, resulted in a touchdown.

Tony Dorsett

One of the great running backs ever, Tony Dorsett retired as the NFL's second all-time rusher. But Tony didn't excel only in the pros. He had a pair of 1,000-yard seasons in high school, four more at the University of Pittsburgh, then five in a row at Dallas. His streak of 11 straight 1,000-yard seasons wasn't stopped by opposing tacklers. On the contrary, it ended in 1982 because of a players' strike. T.D. still led the NFL that year with 745 yards in nine games.

Bo Jackson

Until a severe hip injury put him on the shelf, Bo was the most successful two-sport star in history. An All-Star outfielder for the Kansas City Royals and All-Pro running back for the L.A. Raiders, Bo could do it all. In fact, he set an NFL record as the only back in league history to run for two touchdowns from more than 90 yards out. Bo was simply something special.

NFL
Superstars of the
Past

Many great players have passed through NFL stadiums over the years.

We have already touched on the accomplishments of many of them. Now, here's a brief rundown of some of the best. They can't all be listed, of course, but many of the most memorable are.

Unlike other sports, football has a few "glamour" positions—especially quarterback, running back, and receiver—where stars seem to shine brightest. This list features 49 of football's most outstanding—and best-known—players.

Lance Alworth

"Bambi" 6'0", 184-pound wide receiver. Born August 3, 1940, Houston, Texas. One of the swiftest and most sure-handed deep receivers in history, Alworth made his mark in the old American Football League. Playing with San Diego in the mid-1960s, he led the AFL in catches and yards three times, with a high of 73 catches in 1966 and 1,602 yards and a 23.2 per-catch average in 1965. He finished his career with Dallas in 1972, winding up with 542 catches for 10,266 yards, an 18.9 average, and 85 touchdowns. His per-catch average is the best among the all-time top 20 receivers. Inducted into the Hall of Fame in 1978.

Ottis Anderson

"O.J." 6'2", 225-pound running back. Born November 19, 1957, West Palm Beach, Florida. This great runner retired after being cut prior to the 1993 season. But nothing can dim his great career. He had a sensational rookie debut for the St. Louis Cardinals in 1979, gaining 1,605 yards on 331 carries. A fine inside and outside runner, O.J. had five 1,000-yard seasons with the Cards before going to the Giants in 1986. He turned back the clock in 1989, rushing for 1,000 yards, then gaining 102 more in Super Bowl XXV to win the MVP prize. He retired as the NFL's eighth best all-time rusher, with more than 10,000 yards.

Sammy Baugh

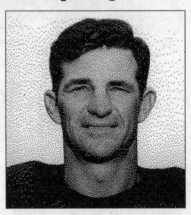

"Slingin Sam" 6'3", 180-pound quarterback. Born March 17, 1914, Temple, Texas. No doubt that Slingin' Sam revolutionized the quarterback position. He is remembered as the first of the modern quarterbacks, a man who used the passing game much as it is used today. Playing with the Washington Redskins from 1937 until 1952, Baugh led the league in passing five times and in 1947 threw for 2,938 yards, an NFL mark that stood until 1963. He also made his presence felt in five championship games. Inducted into the Hall of Fame in 1963.

Chuck Bednarik

"the 60-Minute Man" 6'3", 230-pound center/linebacker. Born May 1, 1925, Bethlehem, Pennsylvania. One of many great football stars to come out of the steel country of Pennsylvania, Bednarik was one of the all-time hard-nosed players. Remembered as the last of the 60-minute men, he thought nothing of going both ways at center and linebacker, and did it in his final game, the 1960 championship contest between his Philadelphia Eagles and the Green Bay Packers. Inducted into the Hall of Fame in 1967.

Raymond Berry

6'2", 187-pound wide receiver. Born February 27, 1933, Corpus Christi, Texas. Simply one of the best ever, a no-frills receiver who worked to make himself the best player he could possibly be. Unitas to Berry was an often unstoppable combination from 1955 to 1967. Berry played a pivotal role on the Colts' title teams of 1958 and 1959 and is one of the NFL's top all-time receivers with 631 catches for 9,275 yards, and 68 touchdowns. He was inducted into the Hall of Fame in 1973 and later coached the New England Patriots.

George Blanda

"Father Time" 6'2", 215-pound quarterback/placekicker. Born September 17, 1927, Youngwood, Pennsylvania. Served as the Oakland Raiders' emergency quarterback and placekicker until he was 48 years old and wound up as pro football's all-time leading scorer, with 2,002 points. Began his pro

Vidalia, Georgia. The cornerstone of the Pittsburgh Steelers' defensive backfield during the team's glory years, Blount was one of the hardest hitters in the game. During his Steeler career he picked off 57 passes, ninth (along with Bobby Boyd) on the all-time list. And like his talented teammates from that era, he earned four Super Bowl rings. Inducted into the Hall of Fame in 1989.

career with the Chicago Bears in 1949 but didn't make his mark until he played with the Houston Oilers of the AFL from 1960 to 1966. Then it was on to the Raiders, where he often performed late-game miracles with both his arm and his leg. Inducted into the Hall of Fame in 1981.

Mel Blount

"Hard Hitter" 6'3", 205-pound cornerback. Born April 10, 1948,

Terry Bradshaw

"Rifle Arm" 6'3", 210-pound quarterback. Born September 2, 1948, Shreveport, Louisiana. A guy who really had the last laugh. Early in his career Bradshaw was ridiculed for not being brainy enough to become a star signal-caller. But Terry always called his own plays and had a wonderfully

strong throwing arm. With talent all around him, he led the Steelers to four Super Bowl triumphs, often completing the big pass with his back against the wall. Since retirement he has acted in films and worked as a football commentator. Inducted into the Hall of Fame in 1989.

Jim Brown

"the Greatest" 6'2", 232-pound fullback. Born February 17, 1936, St. Simons, Georgia. Jim Brown made his pro debut in 1957, yet is still considered the greatest all-around running back ever. Speed, power, and grace, plus a never-say-die attitude made him excel year in and year out. He retired in 1965 while still in his prime to become a movie actor, and he excelled there, too. Still the number four

all-time rusher with 12,312 yards, Jim was an eight-time NFL rushing champ and his 5.2 yards per carry career average is still the best among all the great runners. In nine years he never missed a game. Inducted into the Hall of Fame in 1971.

Dick Butkus

"Mr. Linebacker" 6'3", 245-pound middle linebacker. Born December 9, 1942, Chicago, Illinois. One of the most ferocious players ever, Butkus quickly became the NFL's top middle linebacker when he joined the Bears in 1965. An All-Pro from his rookie year, he terrorized ballcarriers throughout his nine-year career, shortened by a knee injury. To be hit by Dick Butkus was to know you'd been hit. He never gave an inch on the gridiron. Inducted into the Hall of Fame in 1979.

Earl Campbell

"the Tyler Rose" 5'11", 233-pound fullback. Born March 29, 1955, Tyler, Texas. What a runner! Compact and powerful, yet with blazing speed once he was in the open field, Campbell burst onto the scene with the Houston Oilers and ran for a league-leading 1,450 yards in 1978. He was a three-time NFL rushing champ with a personal best of 1,934 yards on 373 carries in 1980. He retired after just eight seasons with 9,407 yards, ninth at that point on the all-time list. In 1980 Earl set an NFL mark by running for more than 200 yards in four different games. Inducted into the Hall of Fame in 1991.

One of the cornerstones of the great Green Bay Packer defense during the team's time of glory, the 1960s. Davis was like the Rock of Gibraltar at end; playing both the run and the pass, he was always one of Vince Lombardi's favorites. Considered a model for the modern defensive end. Inducted into the Hall of Fame in 1981.

Willie Davis

"For the Defense" 6'3", 245-pound defensive end. Born July 24, 1934, Lisbon, Louisiana.

Eric Dickerson

"Running to Daylight" 6'3", 224-pound running back. Born September 2, 1960, Sealy, Texas. Eric Dickerson hasn't always gotten the credit he deserves. He joined the L.A. Rams in 1983 and promptly set a rookie record with 1,808 yards on 390 carries. A year later he broke the all-time

at his own one and ran 99 yards for a touchdown, the longest run from scrimmage in NFL history. He helped the Cowboys win the Super Bowl in his rookie year of 1977, one year after leading the University of Pittsburgh to a national championship. He retired as the league's second all-time rusher with 12,739 yards. Inducted into the Hall of Fame in 1994.

record with 2,105 yards on 379 tries. He had another huge year in 1986 with 1,821 yards. But then he began losing favor and moved to Indianapolis in 1987. The Raiders got him in 1992, and he ran for 729 yards. He left the game in 1993 as a six-time Pro Bowler and the second leading rusher in National Football League history.

Tony Dorsett

"Touchdown Tony" 5'11", 190-pound running back. Born April 7, 1954, Aliquippa, Pennsylvania. Although sometimes underrated, this Dallas Cowboys 1,000-yard rusher was one of the best running backs in NFL history. Dorsett had explosive speed and surprising power for a player his size. On January 3, 1983, in a game against Minnesota, Tony took a handoff

Otto Graham

"Mr. Clutch" 6'1", 195-pound quarterback. Born December 6, 1921, Waukegan, Illinois. One of the all-time greats, Otto Graham helped the Cleveland Browns shock the football world by winning the NFL title in 1950, the first year the team came over from the disbanded All-America Football Conference. An incredibly cool and steady performer,

Graham was also capable of his own brand of magic when necessary. He carried out coach Paul Brown's game plans perfectly and was a fine runner as well as a passer. Always a dangerous third-down thrower. Inducted into the Hall of Fame in 1965.

Joe Greene

"Mean Joe" 6'4", 270-pound defensive tackle. Born September 24, 1946, Temple, Texas. "Mean Joe" was the first player drafted by Chuck Noll when he began rebuilding the Steelers in 1969. After suffering through Pittsburgh's 1-13 season in 1969, Greene prevailed to anchor the "Steel-Curtain Defense" and help the team win four Super Bowls. A rock in the middle, Greene was especially tough against the run but could

also pressure the passer. One of the greats at his position. Inducted into the Hall of Fame in 1987.

John Hannah

"Hog" 6'3", 265-pound offensive guard. Born April 4, 1951, Canton, Georgia. Played for

mostly mediocre New England Patriot teams from 1973 to 1985, yet emerged as perhaps the greatest offensive guard in NFL history. Hannah was strong and tough, a pile-driving blocker who could go straight ahead or pull out on sweeps. He was a rock in the middle, hard to move, tough, resolute. All the qualities needed to play in the trenches. Inducted into the Hall of Fame in 1991.

Franco Harris

"Franco" 6'2", 225-pound fullback. Born March 7, 1950, Fort Dix, New Jersey. No fancy nicknames and no fancy frills to his game. Franco Harris simply played outstanding football for the Pittsburgh Steelers year in and year out. He had power and speed, as well as the ability to

make the big play. It was Harris who was on the receiving end of the famed "immaculate reception" pass from Terry Bradshaw in the opening round of the 1972 playoffs. He is the NFL's fifth all-time rusher with 12,120 yards in 13 seasons. Inducted into the Hall of Fame in 1990.

Paul Hornung

"Golden Boy" 6'2", 220-pound halfback. Born December 23, 1935, Louisville, Kentucky. An All-American quarterback at Notre Dame, Hornung looked like a pro bust at Green Bay until Vince Lombardi converted him to halfback and took advantage of his many talents. Not great at any one thing, he was still a winner. He could follow his outstanding blockers, throw the option pass, and kick field goals, and he smelled the goal line as well as anyone. Hornung set an NFL record with 176 total points in 1960 and was a cornerstone on the great Packer title teams of the 1960s. Inducted into the Hall of Fame in 1986.

Ken Houston

"Kenny" 6'3", 198-pound defensive safety. Born November 12, 1944, Lufkin, Texas. One of the truly great safeties, Kenny Houston starred with both the Houston Oilers and Washington Redskins, playing 14 seasons. A great pass defender and tackler, Houston was also a big threat once he got his hands on the ball. He still holds the NFL mark by taking nine interceptions back for touchdowns during his career, and he did it four times in 1971 alone. Inducted into the Hall of Fame in 1986.

Sam Huff

"Middle Linebacker" 6'1", 230-pound middle linebacker. Born October 4, 1934, Morgantown, West Virginia. Perhaps the first player to define the position of middle linebacker, Huff was the center of a New York Giants defensive unit that captured the fancy of the fans in the mid-1950s. A tough tackler and dogged pursuer, Huff is often remembered for his one-on-one battles with running back Jim Brown. He finished his career with the Redskins in 1969, and was inducted into the Hall of Fame in 1982.

Don Hutson

"Alabama Antelope" 6'1", 180-pound wide receiver. Born January 31, 1913, Pine Bluff, Arkansas. Although he played in another era, with the Packers from 1935 to 1945, there are still those who say Don Hutson was as good as any wide receiver ever. Fast and strong, with an ability to get open, Hutson was a touchdown maker in a time when the pass was not used as often as it is today. He led the NFL in receiving five straight years and was the first to gain more than 1,000 yards receiving in a season. He scored an amazing 105 touchdowns during his career and was inducted into the Hall of Fame in 1963.

David Jones

"Deacon" 6'5", 250-pound defensive end. Born December 9, 1938, Eatonville, Florida. This perennial All-Pro was one of the rocks on the Los Angeles Rams front four known as the "fear-

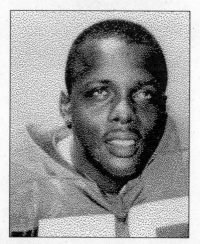

some foursome" in the 1960s. A great pass-rusher, the Deacon was adept at using the head slap, which often left opponents with ears ringing and wondering how Jones got around them. He finished his career with the San Diego Chargers and Washington Redskins. Inducted into the Hall of Fame in 1980.

Sonny Jurgensen

"Jurgy" 6'0", 203-pound quarterback. Born August 23, 1934, Wilmington, North Carolina. If Sonny Jurgensen came up today people would probably say he was too small to play professional football. But, in truth, he was one of the great passers and competitors in National Football League history. Jurgy had a quick and accurate arm, playing 18 seasons for the Philadelphia Eagles and Washington Redskins. He is still the seventh-rated all-time passer, throwing for 32,224 yards and 255 touchdowns. In his great 1967 season, Jurgy threw for 3,747 yards, establishing a record that wasn't broken until 1979. Sonny was simply one of the best ever to play the game. Inducted into the Hall of Fame in 1983.

Jack Lambert

"the Tough Guy" 6'4", 220-pound middle linebacker. Born July 8, 1952, Mantua, Ohio. They said Jack Lambert wasn't big enough to play the middle. Boy, were they wrong. Lambert made up for any lack of bulk with pure toughness and determination, becoming an All-Pro and playing a pivotal role with the Pittsburgh Steelers' "Steel-Curtain Defense" of the 1970s. A never-say-die player who feared nothing, Lambert proudly wears four Super Bowl rings as a tribute to his role with the Steeler dynasty. Inducted into the Hall of Fame in 1990.

Dick Lane

"Night Train" 6'2", 210-pound defensive back. Born April 16, 1928, Austin, Texas. In addition to his terrific nickname, "Night Train" Lane was one of the best defensive backs ever. One of the bigger backs of his time, he played from 1952 to 1965 with the Los Angeles Rams, Chicago Cardinals, and Detroit Lions. Always a threat to intercept, Night Train is third on the all-time list with 68 thefts. He is also second in total yards with returned pickoffs, and lugged five back for scores. Inducted into the Hall of Fame in 1974.

Steve Largent

"Pure Pass-catcher" 5'11", 191-pound wide receiver. Born September 28, 1954, Tulsa, Oklahoma. They said he was too small, wasn't fast enough, wasn't strong enough, wasn't durable enough. Yet when Steve Largent

became one of their first All-Pro players and stayed through 1974, when the team was well into its glory years. Lilly was one of the best, a player who could stop the run and go after the quarterback. A key member of the original "Doomsday Defense," Lilly was an 11-time Pro Bowler and the first man to have his name placed in the famed "Ring of Honor" atop Texas Stadium. Inducted into the Hall of Fame in 1980.

of the Seattle Seahawks retired after 14 seasons in 1989, he was the NFL's all-time leader with 819 catches and 13,089 yards. Both marks have since been surpassed, but second place isn't so bad, either. Largent had the knack of getting open and was blessed with a pair of great hands. He didn't drop many. In another tribute to his talent, he piled up his incredible statistics while playing for mostly mediocre teams. Oh, yes, he also caught an even 100 touchdown passes, another outstanding achievement.

Bob Lilly

"Mr. Cowboy" 6'5", 260-pound defensive tackle. Born July 26, 1939, Olney, Texas. Bob Lilly started with the Dallas Cowboys in 1961, the franchise's second season. He

John Mackey

"Tight End Supreme" 6'2", 224-pound tight end. Born September 24, 1941, New York City. Widely considered the prototype of the modern tight end, John Mackey could do it all on the field. He was big and strong enough to block defensive linemen, had speed to get open and

go deep, and was able to make the tough catch. A Baltimore Colt from 1963 to 1971, Mackey caught many clutch passes from John Unitas, including an 89-yarder against the Rams in 1966. Inducted in the Hall of Fame in 1992.

Gino Marchetti

"Fifties Tough" 6'4", 245-pound defensive end. Born

January 2, 1927, Smithers, West Virginia. One of the toughest and most talented defenders of the 1950s. Marchetti was part of a great Baltimore Colts defensive unit that rivaled that of the New York Giants, the team the Colts beat for a pair of championships in 1958 and 1959. Marchetti used both power and finesse, and was quick enough to chase down ballcarriers. In the great sudden death title game in 1958, Marchetti made a key tackle late in the game. Then, despite the fact that he had fractured his leg, he refused to leave the sideline for treatment until he knew his team had won. Tough. Inducted into the Hall of Fame in 1972.

Hugh McElhenny

"the King" 6'1", 198-pound running back. Born December 31, 1928, Los Angeles, California. One of the great broken-field runners from pro football's earlier days, McElhenny played with the San Francisco 49ers during his peak years. His career lasted from 1952 to 1964, and while he didn't have the big numbers of the backs who followed, he often drove defenders crazy with his side-to-side dashes as he looked for yet another hole in the defense. McElhenny never

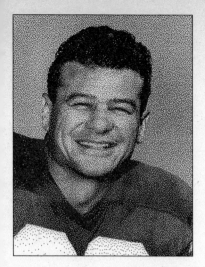

25, 1933, Reading, Pennsylvania. An equal threat as a runner or receiver, Moore could go all the way from any place on the field. Playing for the great Baltimore teams of the late 1950s and early 1960s, he was a favorite target for John Unitas's passes. He still holds the NFL mark for scoring touchdowns in 18 straight games, and was always extremely difficult to bring down in the open field. Inducted into the Hall of Fame in 1975.

Anthony Munoz

led the league in rushing, but he was so well-respected by his peers that he was given the nickname of "the King." Inducted into the Hall of Fame in 1970.

Lenny Moore

"Touchdown" 6'1", 198-pound runner/receiver. Born November

"Tackle Supreme" 6'6", 284-pound offensive tackle. Born August 19, 1958, Ontario, California. Anthony Munoz announced his retirement in 1992, tried a brief comeback in '93, but then retired for good after a pre-season injury. A sure-fire future Hall of Famer, Munoz

was one of the best offensive tackles the game has seen. He went to a record-tying 11 Pro Bowls and was an incredible pass-blocker. Playing a sometimes thankless position, Munoz won nearly all his wars in the trenches after joining the Cincinnati Bengals in 1980.

Joe Namath

"Broadway Joe" 6'2", 200-pound quarterback. Born May 31, 1943, Beaver Falls, Pennsylvania. He didn't have the stats that some of today's quarterbacks have, and his gimpy knees were always making medical news. But Broadway Joe was a winner, a rifle-armed quarterback with a lightning release to strike terror into the hearts of defensive backs. He led the New York Jets to football's greatest

upset in Super Bowl III, and once threw for 496 yards and six touchdowns in a 1972 game against Baltimore. A courageous quarterback who often played while in pain, Namath was inducted into the Hall of Fame in 1985.

Alan Page

"Purple People Eater" 6'4", 225-pound defensive tackle. Born August 7, 1945, Canton, Ohio. Born in the town that houses the Pro Football Hall of Fame, Alan Page always seemed destined for greatness. The anchor of the Minnesota Vikings' front four known as the "Purple People Eaters," Page was a perennial All-Pro performer who often used his incredible quickness to control the line of scrimmage. He played light for a defensive tackle, but did he ever play big. Now a practicing attorney, Page was inducted into the Hall of Fame in 1988.

Walter Payton

"Sweetness" 5'10½", 205-pound running back. Born July 25, 1954, Columbia, Mississippi. What can you say about the NFL's all-time leading rusher except that he was a great player of exceptional drive and character. Walter Payton was a true

scored six in one game against the 49ers, including an 80-yard pass play, 21-yard run, 50-yard run, and 85-yard punt return. He had electricity every time he touched the ball. Because his career was shortened by two knee injuries, Sayers's stats are not among the leaders. But anyone who saw him run with the football knows he is among the elite of all time. Inducted into the Hall of Fame in 1977.

superstar who set a record by rushing for more than 1,000 yards in 10 of his 13 seasons. He wound up with 16,726 yards on a record 3,838 carries. A tough, uncompromising runner, Payton carried the ball as often as asked to, often gaining strength as the game progressed. He drove himself to work hard, even in the off-season, and was always ready to play. The heart of many great Chicago Bears teams, "Sweetness" was inducted into the Hall of Fame in 1993.

Gale Sayers

"the Kansas Comet" 6'0", 200-pound running back. Born May 30, 1943, Wichita, Kansas. Perhaps the greatest open field runner ever, Sayers burst onto the pro scene in 1965, scoring 22 touchdowns for the Bears, many of them on long, brilliant runs. He

O. J. Simpson

"the Juice" 6'1", 212-pound running back. Born July 9, 1947, San Francisco, California. One of the most magnetic runners ever, Simpson first captured the imagination of the public during his days as a star player at the University of Southern California. Playing with a weak Buffalo Bills team, he found his first years in the NFL difficult. Then, in 1973, the Juice became the NFL's first 2,000-yard runner. Blessed with tremendous speed and power and the instincts of the great ones, Simpson wound up the seventh leading rusher ever, with 11,236 yards. His 4.7 career per-carry average is near the top of the list. Inducted into the Hall of Fame in 1985.

Mike Singletary

"Samurai" 6'0", 228-pound middle linebacker. Born October 9, 1958, Houston, Texas. A thoroughly professional middle linebacker, Mike Singletary was all business every time he took the field for the Chicago Bears. The spiritual as well as physical leader of a rugged Bear defense, Singletary was a frequent All-Pro and NFL Defensive Player of the

Year. He was a key man in the Chicago Super Bowl team in 1985, a deadly tackler who was always around the ball. He retired after the 1992 season.

Bart Starr

"True Leader" 6'1", 200-pound quarterback. Born January 9, 1934, Montgomery, Alabama. The quiet and efficient

leader of Vince Lombardi's Green Bay Packer machine of the 1960s, Starr was an accurate and careful passer who became extremely dangerous on third down. He was always protected by his fine ground game but when he had to pass his team to victory, he could. Tough, determined, and still one of the top 20 all-time passers, Starr quarterbacked the Packers to victories in the first two Super Bowls. Inducted into the Hall of Fame in 1977.

Roger Staubach

"Jolly Roger" 6'3", 202-pound quarterback. Born February 5, 1942, Cincinnati, Ohio. An elusive signal-caller with a strong arm, Staubach joined the Dallas Cowboys in 1969 after spending five years in the Navy. He soon

became an All-Pro and one of the most dangerous comeback quarterbacks ever. The Cowboys were never out of a game with the Jolly Roger at the helm. Staubach could also scramble and was extremely tough to bring down. With a quarterback rating of 83.4, he is still ranked as one of the best passers ever. Inducted into the Hall of Fame in 1985.

Fran Tarkenton

"Scrambler" 6'0", 185-pound quarterback. Born February 3, 1940, Richmond, Virginia. Playing for the expansion Minnesota Vikings beginning in 1961, Fran Tarkenton often had to run for his life. But he was good at it, bringing the act of scrambling to high art and breaking the myth that great quarterbacks had to pass from the pocket. He scrambled and passed for 18 years for the Vikings and New York Giants, and when he retired he had thrown and completed more passes for more yards and more touchdowns than any other quarterback in NFL history. So what if his teams lost three Super Bowl games? Fran the Scram could really play. He was inducted into the Hall of Fame in 1986.

Jim Taylor

"Pure Fullback" 6'0", 216-pound fullback. Born September 20, 1935, Baton Rouge, Louisiana. He wasn't as big as some fullbacks, not as fast as others, but Jim Taylor played with a controlled fury that made him one of the very best. The heart of the Green Bay Packer ground attack in the 1960s, Taylor rushed for more than 1,000 yards in five straight seasons. The crew-cutted fullback often preferred running over people rather than around them. Although he played in the shadow of another fullback named Jim, Jim Brown, Taylor ran for 83 touchdowns and gained 8,597 yards. There weren't many who did it better. Inducted into the Hall of Fame in 1976.

Lawrence Taylor

"L.T." 6'3", 245-pound linebacker. Born February 4, 1959, Williamsburg, Virginia. Just say the initials "L.T." That's all it takes to describe perhaps the best linebacker to ever play pro football. Taylor was devastating from his first day as a New York Giant in 1981, and with 126.5

sacks at the end of 1992 he was the all-time leader in that category. As of 1993, Reggie White of Green Bay was the new leader. L.T. was a punishing player who combined blazing speed and quickness with a keen football instinct and great strength. He was often able to take over games nearly single-handedly. A part of the New York Giants winning efforts in Super Bowls XXI and XXV, Taylor changed his mind about retiring after a heel injury ended his 1992 season. He played well in spots during 1993, saw the Giants return to the playoffs, then announced his retirement for good.

record of 47 straight games with a TD toss. Inducted into the Hall of Fame in 1979.

John Unitas

"Johnny U" 6'1", 195-pound quarterback. Born May 7, 1933, Pittsburgh, Pennsylvania. Perhaps the ultimate quarterback success story. Discovered playing sandlot ball after being cut by the Steelers, Johnny U went to Baltimore and became the best of his era, or maybe any era. A prolific passer with an uncanny feel for the passing game, he had tremendous confidence in his ability to move a ballclub. The Colts won a pair of titles under his guidance and he wound up with more than 40,000 passing yards, 290 touchdowns, and that amazing

Steve Van Buren

"Flying Dutchman" 6'1", 200-pound running back. Born December 28, 1920, La Ceiba, Honduras. When Steve Van Buren of the Philadelphia Eagles

gained 1,008 yards in 1947, he was just the second back in NFL history to break the 1,000-yard barrier. Two years later he set another record with 1,146 yards, and it stood until 1958. Considered the first modern running back, Van Buren did it with speed and power. He led the NFL in rushing four times, and in the 1949 title game against the Rams he ran for 196 yards in 31 carries on a drenched and muddy field. Inducted into the Hall of Fame in 1965.

Paul Warfield

"Going Deep" 6'0", 188-pound wide receiver. Born November 28, 1942, Elmira, New York. Still widely considered one of the most dangerous deep receivers in history, Warfield was an All-Pro with both the Cleveland Browns and Miami Dolphins. He often leaped high in the air to make a catch, completely unafraid of the hits he might take. Because of the era and the teams for which he played, Warfield never caught a huge number of passes and went over 1,000 yards receiving just one time in a 13-year career. But he scored 86

touchdowns and was often over 20-yards per catch. Inducted into the Hall of Fame in 1983.

Larry Wilson

"Throwback" 6'0", 190-pound safety. Born March 24, 1938, Rigby, Idaho. A tough and uncompromising defender, Larry Wilson anchored the Cards' backfield with his rough-and-tumble style of play. A throwback who hated to come out of the lineup, he once played with two broken wrists. In 1966, Larry intercepted at least one pass in seven straight games. He retired in 1972 after 13 seasons and with 52 interceptions under his belt. Inducted into the Hall of Fame in 1978.

Willie Wood

"Super Safety" 5'10", 190-pound safety. Born December 23, 1936, Washington, D.C. Fast, tough, a great leaper, and a player with a nose for the football. That describes the All-Pro safety Willie Wood, a fixture in the Green Bay Packers' defensive backfield during the team's glory years in the 1960s. Wood had a knack for the big play, and while he isn't among the top 20 in interceptions, he had some big pickoffs, such as the one he grabbed at the start of the second half of Super Bowl I and took back 50 yards. Inducted into the Hall of Fame in 1989.

11

NFL
Superstars of the
Present

What makes a super-
star? To begin with,
he or she has to have
talent. That goes without saying. But there also has to be
that little something extra.
Superstars must have the ability to control a ballgame, to
elevate their own game and
sometimes carry their team. They also
need the type of personality that attracts
attention and makes the fans want to see
them perform.

There are certainly many excep-
tionally talented players in the National
Football League today. It's sometimes
difficult to separate the stars from the
superstars and those very special elite who
might be called megastars. Here are 29 of
the outstanding performers from the 1990s.

Troy Aikman

"New Dallas Hero" 6'4", 222-pound quarterback. Born November 21, 1966, Cerritos, California. The Most Valuable Player in the 1993 Super Bowl, Aikman has come full circle

since joining the Cowboys in 1989. He went through a 1-15 rebuilding season that year and has matured along with the club. In 1992 Troy was the third leading passer in the league, throwing for 3,445 yards and 23 touchdowns. Against Buffalo in the Super Bowl, Aikman hit on 22 of 30 passes for 273 yards and four touchdowns. The former UCLA All-American is widely considered the best young quarterback in the game.

Morten Andersen

"Kicker Supreme" 6'2", 221-pound placekicker. Born August 19, 1960, Struer, Denmark. This New Orleans Saints left-foot kicker is one of the best ever. Coming into the 1992 season he had a 77.22 percent field-goal accuracy rating, one of the best in NFL history. He can boot them short or long, and cranked out a 60-yarder against the Bears in 1991, the second longest in league annals. In 1992 Andersen hit on 29 of 34 field goals for a league-best 85.3 percent accuracy. He was tied for second in the league in scoring with 120 points. In 1993, he connected on 28 of 35 three-pointers. Outstanding again.

Randall Cunningham

"Eagles Leader" 6'4", 205-pound quarterback. Born March 27, 1963, Santa Barbara, California. One of the most gifted athletes ever to play the quarterback position, Randall Cunningham is capable of greatness every time out. He has also been called reckless and unpredictable. But he has a rocket arm and is also an outstanding runner. In 1990 he threw for 3,466 yards and ran for 942 more, averaging 7.98 yards a carry. In 1991 Cunningham had major knee surgery, but he bounced back to be the fifth best passer in the league in 1992. Joined the Eagles in 1985 and the team hopes he can still lead them to that elusive Super Bowl crown. He missed most of 1993 after suffering a broken leg early in the season.

Richard Dent

"All-Pro Defender" 6'5", 265-pound defensive end. Born December 13, 1960, Atlanta, Georgia. One of the best defensive ends from the mid-1980s to early 1990s, Richard Dent was one of the anchors of the great Chicago Bears defensive units. He was a Pro Bowler in his second season of 1984 and was outstanding in that game with three sacks. A year later he was

the MVP of Super Bowl XX, getting 1.5 sacks and three tackles and forcing two fumbles as the Bears whipped the Patriots. He was still good enough to get 8.5 sacks in 1992. His career sack figures show that he is one of the greatest sackmasters ever, along with the likes of Lawrence Taylor and Reggie White. That's pretty fast company.

John Elway

"Miracle Man" 6'3", 215-pound quarterback. Born June 28, 1960, Port Angeles, Washington. A study in contrasts. Elway can look undisciplined and wild. Sometimes he throws the ball too hard. But 31 times in his Denver Broncos career this incredibly athletic quarterback brought his club from behind in the fourth quarter. He was also the NFL's winningest quarterback from 1984 to 1991 and the only player in NFL history to throw for more than 3,000 yards and rush for more than 200 yards in seven straight seasons. He was the

AFC's leading passer in 1993, throwing for a league best 4,030 yards. There is no one better at bringing a team from behind in the closing seconds of a game.

Darrell Green

"NFL's Fastest Man" 5'8", 170-pound cornerback. Born February 15, 1960, Houston, Texas. The Redskins' speedy defensive back is one of the best coverage men in the league. He made the Pro Bowl for the fifth time in 1991 after leading the Skins with five pickoffs and 21 passes defended. Injuries limited

him to just one pickoff in 1992, but he is still considered a top defender. Had a 52-yard punt return for a TD against Chicago in a 1987 playoff game and has twice won the NFL's Fastest Man competition.

Michael Irvin

"All-Pro Receiver" 6'2", 200-pound wide receiver. Born March 5, 1966, Fort Lauderdale, Florida. Has firmly established himself as one of the top pass receivers in football as well as one of the most valuable Dallas Cowboys. Irvin joined the Boys in 1988 and was on his way to a great year in 1989 when he hurt a knee. He emerged as a force in 1991 with a team-record 93 catches for 1,523 yards, best in the NFL. In 1992, Michael

grabbed 78 passes for 1,396 yards and seven scores. His 17.9 per catch average was one of the highest in the league. A year later, in 1993, he had 88 catches for another 1,330 yards.

Jim Kelly

"Tough Guy" 6'3", 218-pound quarterback. Born February 14,

1960, Pittsburgh, Pennsylvania. One of the finest quarterbacks in football, Jim Kelly must live with the stigma of having guided the Buffalo Bills to four straight Super Bowl appearances (1991-1994), only to see his team lose each time. But Kelly is a talented, tough, and magnetic leader who has the numbers to prove it. After playing two years in the now disbanded United States Football League he joined the Bills in 1986. In 1991 Jim was the top passer in the AFC with 3,844 yards and 33 scores, as well as a 64.1 completion percentage. Injuries slowed him a bit in 1992, but his career quarterback rating has him in the company of Joe Montana and Dan Marino. He proved it again in '93, leading the Bills to a fourth straight appearance in the Super Bowl.

Cortez Kennedy

"the Big Force" 6'3", 293-pound defensive tackle. Born August 23, 1968, Osceola, Arkansas. Rapidly emerging as perhaps the top defensive tackle in the game, Cortez Kennedy had an All-Pro season in 1992. He was up among the leaders in sacks with 14 and also in tackles. Although he started just two games as a rookie in 1990, he began emerging in 1991, lead-

ing the Seahawk linemen with 72 tackles and 6.5 sacks. He has trimmed down from 330 pounds and is getting better with age.

Bernie Kosar

"Sidearmer" 6'5", 215-pound quarterback. Born November 23,

1963, Boardman, Ohio. A quarterback who supposedly does everything wrong, but became one of the best. Kosar is slow, doesn't have a rifle arm, and throws with a strange, sidearm motion. Yet in 1991 he broke one of the NFL's great records, throwing 308 passes without an interception. Injuries and mediocre teams have hurt him in recent years, but Kosar is one of the smartest QBs in the game. He was a starter at age 21 in 1985 and a year later threw for 3,854 yards as the Browns won a divisional title. In 1993, he left the Browns and joined the Dallas Cowboys.

James Lofton

"Speed and Grace" 6'3", 190-pound wide receiver. Born July 5, 1956, Fort Ord, California. In 1991, at the age 35, James

Lofton became the oldest player in NFL history to gain more than 1,000 yards receiving. In 1992 the speedy and graceful wide receiver of the Buffalo Bills gained another 786 yards to become the all-time leader in receiving yards with more than 13,800. He started his brilliant career with the Packers, went to the Raiders in 1987 and signed with the Bills in 1989. A Pro Bowler many times over, Lofton continued to play as a backup in 1993.

Ronnie Lott

"Hard Hitter" 6'0", 205-pound safety. Born May 8, 1959, Albuquerque, New Mexico. In the twilight of a great career, Ronnie Lott has earned the respect and admiration of an entire league. A dominant player since his rookie year of 1981, his ferocious play helped the San Francisco 49ers win four Super Bowls. Joining the Raiders in 1991, he became an All-Pro once again and led the NFL with eight interceptions. He is now among the top ten pickoff men of all time. In 1993 Lott brought his ball-hawking and tackling ability, as well as his leadership, to the New York Jets, and produced yet another fine year.

Nick Lowery

"Mr. Accuracy" 6'4", 189-pound placekicker. Born May 27, 1956, Munich, Germany. The stats make it very clear: Nick Lowery is the most accurate field-goal kicker of all time. Prior to the 1992 season, the veteran Kansas City Chiefs booter had made good on 284 of 358 field-goal tries for an amazing 79.33 percent. Then, in 1992, at the age of 36, Lowery booted an incredible 22 of 24. That's a 91.7 percent accuracy rate. He's now moving up among the all-time scorers, with more than 1,400 career points. A real All-Pro.

Dan Marino

"Pure Passer" 6'4", 224-pound quarterback. Born September 15, 1961, Pittsburgh,

Pennsylvania. A star from the first day he put on a Miami Dolphin uniform in 1983, Dan Marino is a multiple record-setting passer who is already being called the best ever in some circles. Not only is he the second highest-rated passer in history, but all his lifetime numbers are at or near the top. In 1984 he became the first NFL signal-caller to throw for more than 5,000 yards in a season. He also set a mark with 48 touchdown passes that year, and at the end of 1992 he was tied with John Unitas for second place with 290 career TD tosses. He moved into second place early in 1993 before a torn achilles tendon sidelined him for the year. It was the first major injury of his career.

Jim McMahon

"Mr. Cool" 6'1", 190-pound quarterback. Born August 21, 1959, Jersey City, New Jersey. Jim McMahon doesn't have the

natural talent or the numbers of other top quarterbacks. But his magnetic personality and ability to win big games has always made him a superstar. His career peaked with the Bears in 1985 when he led the team to an NFC title and Super Bowl championship. But injuries have always hampered him, causing him to miss sizable portions of several seasons. He spent a couple of years as a backup in Philadelphia before coming to the Minnesota Vikings. Jim was the NFC Rookie of the Year with the Bears back in 1982, and he led the Vikings into the playoffs in 1993.

Art Monk

"All-Time Receiving Champ"
6'3", 210-pound wide receiver.
Born December 5, 1957, White
Plains, New York. Quiet, unas-
suming, and simply great: that
describes Art Monk who, in
1992, became the NFL's all-time
receiving champ with a total of
847 catches since joining the
Washington Redskins in 1980.
Monk surpassed Steve Largent,
who had 819. The former
Syracuse star has been an
incredibly consistent performer,
a big receiver who can make the
tough catches in traffic and who
is an outstanding runner after
getting the ball. He has been an
integral part of the Skins' outstanding teams throughout the
1980s and into the 1990s. A
real All-Pro. He continued to add
to his records in 1993.

Joe Montana

"Comeback Kid" 6'1", 195-
pound quarterback. Born June
11, 1956, New Eagle,
Pennsylvania. Even if Joe
Montana never throws another
pass he will retire as the highest-
rated passer of all time. He will
also retire as an All-Pro who led
the San Francisco 49ers to four
Super Bowl championships. In
the eyes of many, Montana is
the best. His accuracy is incredible, his instinct for the passing
game is uncanny, and his ability
to bring a team from behind is
unsurpassed. He is the Super
Bowl's only three-time Most
Valuable Player. Elbow surgery
kept him out almost all of 1992,
but he came back strong with
the Kansas City Chiefs in 1993,
leading them all the way to the
AFC title game. Among his

records is the highest completion percentage in history, nearly 64 percent.

Warren Moon

"Rifle Arm" 6'3", 212-pound quarterback. Born November 18, 1956, Los Angeles, California. It has been a great career for Warren Moon. He started in the Canadian Football League, where he led the Edmonton Eskimos to five Grey Cup championships. When he came south to the Houston Oilers in 1984, he quickly put his name in the NFL record book. A scrambler with a rifle arm, Warren set a record with 655 pass attempts in 1991 and 404 completions that same year. He and Dan Marino are the only quarterbacks to put together back-to-back 4,000-yard seasons. This Pro Bowler was the league's

fourth best passer in 1992 and once again led the Oilers to the playoffs in 1993.

Jerry Rice

"Touchdown Maker" 6'2", 200-pound wide receiver. Born October 13, 1962, Starkville, Mississippi. Longtime 49er Jerry Rice is the man when it comes to wide receivers. With each year, more people are calling him the best ever at his position. Fast, strong, and with great hands, he is a threat to go all the way every time he catches a pass. In fact, his 10 TD catches in 1992 gave him an all-time NFL record of 103, and he's still going strong. He's already had seven 1,000-yard seasons, with a personal best of 1,570 yards in 1986. With everything else, he was the Super Bowl XXIII MVP and the NFL Player of the Year in the strike-shortened 1987 season when he caught an incredible 22 touchdown passes in just 12 games. In 1993, Rice caught another 98 passes for 1,503 yards while adding to his record with another 15 touchdowns.

Barry Sanders

"Pure Runner" 5'8", 203-pound running back. Born July 16, 1968, Wichita, Kansas. From the time he gained 1,470 yards as a rookie with the Detroit Lions in 1989, Barry Sanders hasn't looked back. Quick, strong, compact, and fast, he is perhaps the best pure runner in football. He hasn't been blessed with a great team around him, but he led the NFL with 1,304 yards in 1990. He nailed 1,548 yards in 1991 and another 1,352 in 1992. No one can stop this guy. Though a

knee injury slowed him in '93, he's going to run all the way to the Hall of Fame.

Junior Seau

"Pro Bowl Backer" 6'3", 250-pound linebacker. Born January 19, 1969, American Samoa. Junior Seau reached Pro Bowl status with the San Diego Chargers the old fashioned way: he worked hard. A big, strong inside backer with astonishing 4.61-second speed running the 40-yard dash, he has also been described as a "maniac" in the weight room. Had 129 tackles and seven sacks in a Pro-Bowl season of 1991 and then became the only AFC unanimous Pro-Bowl choice in 1992, leading the league in tackles behind the line of scrimmage. Plays hurt and doesn't like teammates who don't.

Sterling Sharpe

"Record-Breaking Receiver"
6'1", 205-pound wide receiver. Born April 6, 1965, Glenville, Georgia. Sharpe made news in 1992 when he caught 108 passes for the Green Bay Packers, breaking the single-season record set by Art Monk in 1984. In 1989 Sharpe grabbed 90 passes for 1,423 yards. Already a three-time Pro Bowler, he has become the prime target in the improving Packer pass offense. The only thing he doesn't have is blazing downfield speed, but that obviously hasn't hurt him very much. Not when you catch 108 passes in one year, then come back the next and break your record with 112 catches, as Sharpe did in 1992 and 1993.

Bruce Smith

"Dominating Defender"
6'4", 275-pound defensive end. Born June 18, 1963, Norfolk, Virginia. With 14 sacks in 1992, the Buffalo Bills' Bruce Smith reestablished himself as one of the best defensive ends in the NFL. His 1991 season was disrupted by a knee injury after he had become a superstar with a sensational campaign that saw him named the NFL's Defensive Player of the Year by the Associated Press. Described as an "attack player," he has become tougher at playing the run in recent years. He had another All-Pro year in '93, adding 13.5 sacks to his ledger.

Emmitt Smith

"Rushing Champ" 5'9", 203-pound running back. Born May 15, 1969, Pensacola, Florida. A three-time rushing champion after just four years in the league, Emmitt Smith was a big part of the Dallas Cowboys' Super Bowl-winning effort in 1992, leading the NFL with 1,713 yards on 373 carries for a 4.6 average. This after gaining 1,563 yards on 365 carries the year before. Offensive Rookie of the Year in 1990, Smith has always been extremely durable and injury-free. He doesn't have blazing speed but is close to a genius at following blockers and picking holes. He proved it again in '93, becoming the league's Most Valuable Player while gaining 1,486 yards.

Pat Swilling

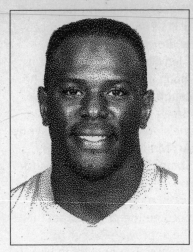

"Swift Sacker" 6'3", 242-pound linebacker. Born October 25, 1964, Taccoa, Georgia. This top-flight outside linebacker had something to prove in 1993 after being traded from New Orleans to Detroit. Once again he was outstanding. As a fifth-year pro in 1991, Pat led the NFL with 17 sacks and was named Defensive Player of the Year by the Associated Press. He slipped to 10.5 sacks in 1992 and it may be necessary for him to turn it up a notch to regain his 1991 status. He was good enough then for some to say he had surpassed the great Lawrence Taylor as the best outside linebacker in the game.

Thurman Thomas

"All-Purpose Superstar"
5'10", 198-pound running back. Born April 16, 1966, Houston, Texas. Had a typical Thurman Thomas year in 1992. The Buffalo Bill All-Pro rushed for 1,487 yards on 312 carries and caught 58 passes for another 626 yards. In 1991 it was 1,407 yards rushing and 631 catching. How's that for consistency? Thomas was also the league MVP in 1991 and is considered the best all-purpose back in the NFL. He's also a fine blocker and has been instrumental in helping the Bills to four straight Super Bowl appearances beginning in January 1991. He ran for another 1,315 yards in '93, best in the AFC.

Reggie White

"Minister of Defense" 6'5", 285-pound defensive end. Born December 19, 1961, Chattanooga, Tennessee. A massive All-Pro player who moved from the Philadelphia Eagles to Green Bay Packers in 1993. White received a huge free-agent contract but earned it with his outstanding play. Through the 1993 season, Reggie had 137 sacks in 137 games. Amazing. During the strike-shortened 1987 season Reggie had 21 sacks in just 12 games. An extremely strong player who has never missed a game to injury, he excels at both rushing the passer and playing the run. An ordained Baptist minister off the field. Hence, his nickname.

Rod Woodson

"Steeler Stalwart" 6'0", 197-pound cornerback. Born March 10, 1965, Fort Wayne, Indiana. Woodson is a very strong and punishing cornerback who's also fast enough to be one of the league's best return specialists. He is a perennial Pro Bowler and has been Steeler MVP twice. He was the league's fourth best punt returner and also had four interceptions in 1992. In '93, he was again an All-Pro and picked off another 8 passes. A fine all-around athlete, Rod qualified for the Olympic trials in the 100-meter high hurdles in 1988. His quickness makes him outstanding on man-to-man coverage.

Steve Young

"MVP" 6'2", 200-pound quarterback. Born October 11, 1961, Salt Lake City, Utah. A backup to Joe Montana with the 49ers

for several years, Young got his chance in 1991 and played enough to lead all quarterbacks with a 101.8 rating. He threw for 17 scores with only 8 interceptions. In 1992, he played full-time and not only led all quarterbacks with a 107 rating, but was the league's Most Valuable Player as well. The southpaw thrower had a brilliant season to take his place among the top signal-callers in football. He also rushed for 537 yards, giving his game yet another dimension. In 1993, he was one of only two NFL quarterbacks to throw for more than 4,000 yards.

12

Coaches'
Records and Other
NFL Numbers

Here's a quick look at the 12 winningest NFL coaches down through the years, listed in order of career victories. Some are names from the past, others from today. Many of them have already been mentioned in other sections of this book. The records include postseason play.

1. Don Shula

The granite-jawed Don Shula started as a coach with the Baltimore Colts but has spent most of his 30-year career behind the Miami Dolphins' bench. A winner all the way, Shula has now directed 327 victories through 1993, lost 158, and tied 6.

2. George Halas

Coached the Chicago Bears for 40 years through thick and thin. No one could fire him because he also owned the team. At the same time, he won more games than anyone else—until Shula broke his record in 1993. His teams won 324, lost 151, and tied 31.

3. Tom Landry

Dallas Cowboys coach Tom Landry

Landry was the first coach of the Dallas Cowboys, staying at the helm for 29 years, until Jerry Jones bought the team in 1989 and hired Jimmy Johnson to take over. But Landry will always be a legend in Dallas, his teams having won 270 games, lost 178, and tied 6.

4. Earl Lambeau

A name from the past, "Curly" Lambeau founded the Green Bay Packers and spent most of his coaching career there. He ended up directing the Chicago Cardinals and Washington Redskins for short stints. His final coaching mark was 229 victories, 134 losses, and 22 ties.

5. Chuck Noll

Noll was the coach of the Pittsburgh Steelers for 23 years. He brought the team up from the basement to win four Super Bowls in the 1970s, then stayed on through the up-and-down 1980s. His final coaching mark was 209 victories, 156 defeats, and 1 tie.

6. Chuck Knox

Chuck Knox has been a traveling man. He has coached for 24 years, directing the Los Angeles Rams, Buffalo Bills, Seattle Seahawks, and then the Rams again. He has been successful everywhere, and his coaching record through 1993 stands at 194-157-1.

7. Paul Brown

Brown is still considered an innovator and a coaching genius. He started with the Cleveland Browns in the old All-America Conference, then brought the Browns into the NFL. Later he was coach and owner of the Cincinnati Bengals. In 21 years of NFL coaching, Brown's teams won 170, lost 108, and tied 6.

8. Bud Grant

Bud Grant rarely showed emotion on the sideline. But his teams did. He directed some Minnesota Vikings ballclubs that were almost always winners. Unfortunately, all four teams that Grant took to the Super Bowl lost. His final coaching record is an impressive 168-108-5.

9. Steve Owen

Owen is another name from the past. He directed the New York Giants for 23 successful years from 1931 to 1953. Old timers remember how good his teams were. Under Owen, the Giants won 153, lost 108, and tied 17.

10. Joe Gibbs

Considered by many a real coaching genius, Joe Gibbs spent 11 years behind the bench of the Washington Redskins before retiring unexpectedly after the 1992 season. His teams won 139 games, lost only 64, and never played a tie.

11. Hank Stram

Stram coached the Kansas City Chiefs and New Orleans Saints for 17 years. His Chiefs team won Super Bowl IV, the high point in Stram's coaching career. His final record before he became a fine football analyst was 136-100-10.

12. Weeb Ewbank

Ewbank had a successful 20-year coaching career with the Baltimore Colts and New York Jets. He was on the sidelines when the Colts whipped the Giants in that epic sudden-death title game in 1958 and again when the Jets upset the mighty Colts in Super Bowl III. His final mark was 134 victories, 130 defeats, and 7 ties.

Four of the most successful and well-known coaches in NFL history are not among those listed above. That's because they coached for shorter times and thus piled up fewer wins. But it's worth mentioning them here.

John Madden

You don't have to be a football fan to have heard of John Madden, who has become a very successful TV analyst and personality. He is also the author of several humorous books about his football career. He coached the Oakland Raiders for a decade, won a Super Bowl title in January 1977, and finished with a record of 112-39-7 for an outstanding winning percentage of .731.

Mike Ditka

The explosive coach of the Chicago Bears might be best remembered for his sideline temper tantrums. No doubt Ditka was intense. He was a great tight end for the Bears and expected his players to give 100 percent every time out. His team won Super Bowl XX, and his 11-year record shows 112 wins, 68 losses, and not a single tie.

Vince Lombardi

A legend everywhere. Lombardi is still thought of as perhaps the greatest coach and motivator ever. His Green Bay Packer teams won five NFL championships, six division titles, and the first two Super Bowls. He moved to Washington, where he coached one year before the cancer that led to his death was diagnosed. In 10 years of coaching, Lombardi won 105 games, lost just 35, and tied 6. His winning percentage of .740 is the best among coaches who have won at least 100 games.

Bill Walsh

Another coach sometimes given the tag "genius," Bill Walsh took over a downtrodden San Francisco 49ers team and drove them to three Super Bowl titles in 10 years. Both Walsh and Chuck Noll were inducted into the Pro Football Hall of Fame in 1993. Walsh's coaching record for 10 years was 102 victories, 63 defeats, and a single tie.

How has your favorite team fared since it has been in the NFL? Here's a quick look at the total records of each of the current 28 teams. Check it out to see what your club has done over the years. The teams are listed in alphabetical order in their conference. Records include the 1993 season.

NFL Team Records

Team	In NFL Since	Won	Lost	Tied
AFC (includes AFL)				
Buffalo Bills	1960	234	257	8
Cincinnati Bengals	1968	182	205	1
Cleveland Browns	1950	358	250	10
Denver Broncos	1960	241	249	10
Houston Oilers	1960	234	260	6
Indianapolis Colts	1953	281	294	7
Kansas City Chiefs	1960	255	233	12
Los Angeles Raiders	1960	304	185	11
Miami Dolphins	1966	253	159	4
New England Patriots	1960	221	270	9
New York Jets	1960	221	271	8
Pittsburgh Steelers	1933	369	400	19
San Diego Chargers	1960	245	244	11
Seattle Seahawks	1976	127	149	0
NFC				
Atlanta Falcons	1966	156	255	5
Chicago Bears	1920	573	371	42
Dallas Cowboys	1960	294	198	6
Detroit Lions	1930	402	416	32
Green Bay Packers	1921	494	422	36
Los Angeles Rams	1937	394	337	20
Minnesota Vikings	1961	262	215	9
New Orleans Saints	1967	160	237	5
New York Giants	1925	493	396	32
Philadelphia Eagles	1933	349	421	23
Phoenix Cardinals	1920	383	514	39
San Francisco 49ers	1950	332	273	13
Tampa Bay Buccaneers	1976	81	194	1
Washington Redskins	1932	430	362	26

We've touched briefly on some of the higher scoring games in NFL history. Now here is the official list of games in which the winning team scored 60 or more points. And since NFL games consist of four 15-minute quarters, for a total of 60 minutes, a 60-point game is a point a minute. No easy feat, indeed.

Scoring Sixty or More

Regular Season (home team in caps)	Date of Game
WASHINGTON 72, New York Giants 41	November 27, 1966
LOS ANGELES RAMS 70, Baltimore 27	October 22, 1950
Chicago Cardinals 65, NEW YORK BULLDOGS 20	November 13, 1949
LOS ANGELES RAMS 65, Detroit 24	October 29, 1950
PHILADELPHIA 64, Cincinnati 0	November 6, 1934
CHICAGO CARDINALS 63, New York Giants 35	October 17, 1948
AKRON 62, Oorang Indians 0	October 29, 1922
PITTSBURGH 62, New York Giants 7	November 30, 1952
CLEVELAND 62, New York Giants 14	December 6, 1953
CLEVELAND 62, Washington 3	November 7, 1954
NEW YORK GIANTS 62, Philadelphia 10	November 26, 1972
Atlanta 62, NEW ORLEANS 7	September 16, 1973
NEW YORK JETS 62, Tampa Bay 28	November 17, 1985
CHICAGO BEARS 61, San Francisco 20	December 12, 1965
Cincinnati 61, HOUSTON 17	December 17, 1972
CHICAGO BEARS 61, Green Bay 7	December 7, 1980
Cincinnati 61, HOUSTON 7	December 17, 1989
ROCK ISLAND 60, Evansville 0	October 15, 1922
CHICAGO CARDINALS 60, Rochester 0	October 7, 1923

Postseason

Chicago Bears 73, WASHINGTON 0	December 8, 1940

Blowouts like that don't happen too often. There have been only 20 of them in more than 70 years. But a look at the numbers shows one thing: the home team is much more likely to produce a huge score. In the 20 games in which the winning team scored 60 or more points, that team was playing at home 16 times.

WHAT HAPPENS WHEN A GAME GOES INTO OVERTIME?

Before 1974, regular-season games that ended in a tie after regulation play were simply tie games. But in 1974 the NFL decided to let the teams play one 15-minute sudden-death overtime period, with the first team to score winning. The game would end in a tie only if neither team could score during the overtime period.

From 1974 through the 1991 season, there were 184 overtime games in the NFL. Here are the numbers to show how the games ended. Note: they are all regular-season games. Playoffs and title games must continue until there is a winner.

How Did They End?

✓ **136 times** both teams had at least one possession in OT.

✓ **48 times** the team that won the coin toss drove for the winning score.

✓ **88 times** the team that won the coin toss won the game.

✓ **83 times** the team that lost the coin toss won the game.

✓ **13 games** ended in a tie.

✓ **119 games** were decided by a field goal.

✓ **51 games** were decided by a touchdown.

✓ **1 game** was decided by a safety.

The last tie game in the NFL was on November 19, 1989, when Cleveland and Kansas City played to a 10-10 deadlock.

Shortest Overtime Games

- 0:21 — Chicago 23, Detroit 17 (11/27/80); kickoff returned for TD
- 0:30 — Baltimore 29, New England 23 (9/4/83)
- 0:55 — New York Giants 16, Philadelphia 10 (9/29/85)

Longest Overtime Games (all postseason)

- 22:40 — Miami 27, Kansas City 24 (12/25/71)
- 17:54 — Dallas Texans 20, Houston 17 (12/23/62)
- 17:02 — Cleveland 23, New York Jets 20 (1/3/87)

NUMBER-ONE DRAFT PICKS

Every year since 1936, the National Football League has held a draft to pick the top college players who are entering the pros. Here are the number-one picks from 1936 to 1993, the NFL team that chose them, their position, and the college from which they came.

From 1961 to 1966, both the AFL and NFL made draft choices. See how many names you remember.

#1 Draft Picks

Season	Pro Team	Player	Position	College
1936	Philadelphia	Jay Berwanger	HB	Chicago
1937	Philadelphia	Sam Francis	FB	Nebraska
1938	Cleveland Rams	Corbett Davis	FB	Indiana
1939	Chicago Cards	Ki Aldrich	C	Texas Christian
1940	Chicago Cards	George Cafego	HB	Tennessee
1941	Chicago Bears	Tom Harmon	HB	Michigan
1942	Pittsburgh	Bill Dudley	HB	Virginia
1943	Detroit	Frank Sinkwich	HB	Georgia
1944	Boston Yanks	Angelo Bertelli	QB	Notre Dame
1945	Chicago Cards	Charley Trippi	HB	Georgia
1946	Boston Yanks	Frank Dancewicz	QB	Notre Dame
1947	Chicago Bears	Bob Fenimore	HB	Oklahoma A&M
1948	Washington	Harry Gilmer	QB	Alabama
1949	Philadelphia	Chuck Bednarik	C	Pennsylvania
1950	Detroit	Leon Hart	E	Notre Dame
1951	N.Y. Giants	Kyle Rote	HB	Southern Methodist
1952	Los Angeles Rams	Bill Wade	QB	Vanderbilt
1953	San Francisco	Harry Babcock	E	Georgia
1954	Cleveland	Bobby Garrett	QB	Stanford
1955	Baltimore	George Shaw	QB	Oregon
1956	Pittsburgh	Gary Glick	DB	Colorado A&M
1957	Green Bay	Paul Hornung	QB	Notre Dame
1958	Chicago Cards	King Hill	QB	Rice
1959	Green Bay	Randy Duncan	QB	Iowa
1960	Los Angeles Rams	Billy Cannon	RB	Louisiana State

#1 Draft Picks

(continued)

Season	Pro Team	Player	Position	College
1961	Minnesota (NFL)	Tommy Mason	RB	Tulane
	Buffalo (AFL)	Ken Rice	G	Auburn
1962	Washington (NFL)	Ernie Davis	RB	Syracuse
	Oakland (AFL)	Roman Gabriel	QB	N.C. State
1963	L.A. Rams (NFL)	Terry Baker	QB	Oregon State
	Kan. City (AFL)	Buck Buchanan	DT	Grambling
1964	San Francisco (NFL)	Dave Parks	E	Texas Tech
	Boston (AFL)	Jack Concannon	QB	Boston College
1965	N.Y. Giants (NFL)	Tucker Frederickson	RB	Auburn
	Houston (AFL)	Larry Elkins	E	Baylor
1966	Atlanta (NFL)	Tommy Nobis	LB	Texas
	Miami (AFL)	Jim Grabowski	RB	Illinois
1967	Baltimore	Bubba Smith	DT	Michigan State
1968	Minnesota	Ron Yary	OT	Southern Cal
1969	Buffalo	O. J. Simpson	RB	Southern Cal
1970	Pittsburgh	Terry Bradshaw	QB	Louisiana Tech
1971	New England	Jim Plunkett	QB	Stanford
1972	Buffalo	Walt Patulski	DE	Notre Dame
1973	Houston	John Matuszak	DE	Tampa
1974	Dallas	Ed Jones	DE	Tenn State
1975	Atlanta	Steve Bartkowski	QB	California
1976	Tampa Bay	Lee Roy Selmon	DE	Oklahoma
1977	Tampa Bay	Ricky Bell	RB	Southern Cal
1978	Houston	Earl Campbell	RB	Texas
1979	Buffalo	Tom Cousineau	LB	Ohio State
1980	Detroit	Billy Sims	RB	Oklahoma

#1 Draft Picks

(continued)

Season	Pro Team	Player	Position	College
1981	New Orleans	George Rogers	RB	South Carolina
1982	New England	Kenneth Sims	DT	Texas
1983	Baltimore	John Elway	QB	Stanford
1984	New England	Irving Fryar	WR	Nebraska
1985	Buffalo	Bruce Smith	DE	Virginia Tech
1986	Tampa Bay	Bo Jackson	RB	Auburn
1987	Tampa Bay	Vinny Testaverde	QB	Miami
1988	Atlanta	Aundray Bruce	LB	Auburn
1989	Dallas	Troy Aikman	QB	UCLA
1990	Indianapolis	Jeff George	QB	Illinois
1991	Dallas	Russell Maryland	DT	Miami
1992	Indianapolis	Steve Emtman	DT	Washington
1993	New England	Drew Bledsoe	QB	Washington State

It's an interesting list. A team with a number-one pick is hoping to select a man who will become an impact player; with luck, even a superstar. Some teams want to fill a particular hole. But a close look at this list of 64 names reveals some interesting facts.

The two positions that dominate by far are running back and quarterback. There were 22 running backs and 19 quarterbacks chosen as number-one picks. That's 41 of the 64 choices. There were only five pass receivers, five defensive tackles, and five defensive ends. The remaining spots went to three linebackers, two centers, one guard, one offensive tackle, and one defensive back.

Interestingly enough, the quarterbacks and running backs are probably the most visible players on the team, the so-called glamour positions. The different teams down through the years seem to feel that these are also the most important positions to which to draft a big name.

But being a number-one pick doesn't guarantee success. Perhaps a little more than half of the picks—about 36 of them—went on to become true impact players. Of those, perhaps 15 could be called superstars. And not all of them were the quarterbacks and running backs.

Number-one picks who became or are potential superstars are Bill Dudley, Chuck Bednarik, Paul Hornung, Roman Gabriel, Buck Buchanan, Tommy Nobis, Bubba Smith, Ron Yary, O. J. Simpson, Terry Bradshaw, Ed "Too Tall" Jones, Earl Campbell, Billy Sims, Bruce Smith, and Troy Aikman.

What does it all prove? That there is no such thing as a sure thing. "Can't miss" prospects can miss. All the top football minds in the country can search the colleges for the best talent, but how their choices perform in the pros owes a great deal to "intangibles" like good fortune, a proper fit between team and player, and the ability of a college star to shine as brightly in the pro game.

13

The Canadian Game

At first glance it looks just like American football. But watch it for a while. Canadian football is a fast, explosive game played on a large field and with some definite differences from its American counterpart. The Canadian Football League (CFL) might be considered just a distant cousin to the National Football League, but it is a league with its own identity and style of play.

INTRODUCING
THE CFL

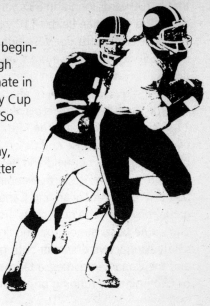

The CFL plays an 18-game schedule beginning in early July and running through
early November. The playoffs culminate in
the championship game for the Grey Cup
trophy the final week in November. So
the schedule begins and ends much
earlier than the NFL season. That way,
the teams can avoid much of the bitter
Canadian winter.

Though Canadian games, for
the most part, are played in smaller
stadiums and before smaller
crowds than those of the NFL, the
league has been extremely stable.
The present two-division structure
began in 1936 with seven teams
participating. The league expanded to eight teams in 1949 and to nine
in 1954. It went back to eight in 1987 when the Montreal team fold-
ed, but in 1993 returned to a nine-team format by adding the
Sacramento (California) Gold Miners, the first United States-based
team to play Canadian football. In early 1994, the CFL announced
plans for expansion teams in Las Vegas, Baltimore, and Shreveport,
Louisiana. All three teams were scheduled to begin play in the 1994
season. This would raise the total number of teams in the league to 12
and mark a major expansion into the United States.

In 1993, Sacramento played in the Western Division. The other teams
in that division were the British Columbia Lions, Calgary Stampeders,
Edmonton Eskimos, and Saskatchewan Roughriders. The Eastern Division
teams were the Hamilton Tiger-Cats, Ottawa Rough Riders, Toronto
Argonauts, and Winnipeg Blue Bombers. Pretty nifty names.

THE RULES TO PLAY BY

Let's take a look at the major rule variations that make Canadian football a different game from its American counterpart. The clearest way
to do this is to simply compare the various parts of the game.

The Canadian field is bigger. American football is played on a field that is 100 yards long and 53⅓ yards wide. Each end zone is 10 yards deep. The Canadian field is 110 yards long and 65 yards wide. Each end zone is 20 yards deep. To put it in perspective, the Canadian field has 3,350 square yards more than the American field. There is an additional 11⅔ yards sideline to sideline, which points up the need for speed and quickness in the Canadian game.

The Canadian game is played with 12 men to a side instead of the 11 in American football. The 12th man is usually an extra backfield player on both offense and defense. The additional player is needed because of the larger field and helps to open the game up on offense.

A touchdown is worth six points and field goals count three points in both American and Canadian football. In the Canadian game, however, the goal posts are on the goal line. In the American game, the posts are on the end line at the rear of the end zone. A safety counts two points in both games. Also in both the American and the Canadian games, a team may score one extra point by kicking or two points by running or passing the ball into the end zone following a touchdown. For the con-version attempt in the American game the ball is placed at the two-yard line. In the Canadian game it is placed at the five-yard line.

In the Canadian game, a team can score a single point by means of a rouge. The rouge is scored by the kicking team when a punt or missed field goal is fielded by a defensive player in the end zone and that player is tackled before he can run the ball out of the end zone. It is also scored by the kicking team when a punt or missed field goal goes out of bounds in the end zone. This rule does not exist in American football.

In American football, the offensive and defensive lines of scrimmage are at each end of the football. In the Canadian game the offensive line of scrimmage is at the forward point of the football, but the defensive line of scrimmage is one yard behind the point of the ball. So in the CFL, a greater distance separates the offensive and defensive lines.

When a Canadian team moves the ball, it has three downs to make 10 yards for a first down. In the American game, the offensive team has four downs in which to make 10 yards. So in the Canadian game the so-called kicking down for the punter is on third down. That's another reason the offense must strike quickly. It's harder to grind out first downs than it is in American football.

A fair catch of a punt is not permitted in Canadian football. Every punt must be run back, and to allow for that tacklers must remain at least five yards from the punt returner until he has touched the ball.

Before the ball is snapped from the center to the quarterback in American football, only one backfield member may be in motion. And he can move only backward or sideways (laterally), never forward. If he moves forward before the snap, a penalty is called. In the Canadian game, any or all players in the backfield may be in motion in any direction before the ball is snapped to the quarterback.

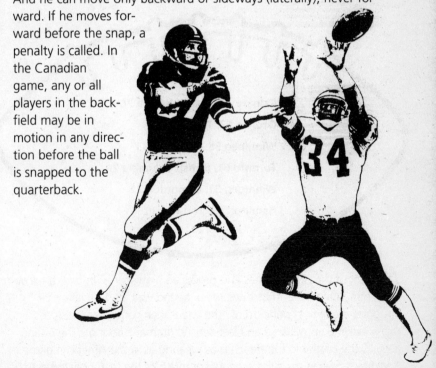

Each quarter of the Canadian game must end with a play. The clock cannot run out between plays as it often does in the American game. Even with no time left, a final play must be run.

In the Canadian game, the hash marks are 24 yards in from each sideline, leaving 17 yards in the middle between the marks. In American football, the hash marks are placed in line with the uprights of the goal posts. That gives American kickers practically a dead-on shot at a field goal. Canadian kickers often have to boot the ball from five yards outside the posts, a much tougher angle.

The rules of the Canadian game indicate differences in strategy. With just three downs to make ten yards, Canadian offenses must emphasize quick-striking plays that will eat up yardage. Three-yard and four-yard running plays aren't good enough. There is a great deal of passing and a lot of running to the outside, taking advantage of the increased size of the field.

The result is a wide-open game with generally higher scores than in American football. A random look at the first three weeks of the 1992 CFL season turned up the following results:

Calgary 44, Saskatchewan 26

Ottawa 53, Toronto 42

Winnipeg 36, Hamilton 33

Toronto 61, British Columbia 20

Winnipeg 51, Edmonton 32

Hamilton 39, Toronto 30

Most of the other games also produced high scores. In fact, the lowest-scoring game over that three-week period was 23-13. Defensive struggles are almost unheard of. The wide-open game also produces many exciting comebacks and last-second dramatic finishes. The hitting is hard, the battles in the trenches as wearing as in the American game. The differences in the rules account for much of the fast, nonstop action.

THE CFL BY THE NUMBERS

Where do the CFL players come from? Some are native Canadians who play collegiate football in either Canada or the United States. Others are American players who decide to play north of the border for any number of reasons, including a desire to get more playing experience before moving to the NFL or the failure to make an NFL squad. A few simply get offers they can't refuse from the Canadian league. There are also some American football players who threaten to play in the CFL if their contract demands are not met, and then follow through on the threat.

Canadian teams, however, are limited in the number of non-Canadian players that they can accept. According to the CFL rule book, the roster of each team shall consist of 14 imports, 20 non-imports,

and three quarterbacks. An "import" is a player who played football outside of Canada and who did not play football in Canada prior to his 17th birthday. A "non-import" is a player who has spent a total of five of his first 15 years in Canada or who has never played football outside of Canada.

The rule allows each team to keep a Canadian flavor and prevents clubs from signing a team of "ringers" from the United States. In other words, it makes sure that the good Canadian players get a chance to play their own game.

CFL RECORD BREAKERS

Individual records in the CFL are just as impressive as those of the NFL. The names of most record setters may not be familiar to American football fans, but these players' achievements are definitely "major league." Let's take a quick look at a few of the best.

Willie Burton of Calgary set the CFL single-season rushing mark when he gained 1,896 yards on 332 carries in 1975. That's an average of 5.7 yards per carry. Eric Dickerson holds the NFL mark with 2,105 yards in 1984.

The CFL career-rushing leader is George Reed, who played for Saskatchewan for 13 seasons between 1963 and 1975. Reed, a fullback, gained 16,116 yards on 3,243 workhorse carries. He averaged 5.0 yards per carry for his career and scored a record 134 touchdowns. Walter Payton holds the NFL record with 16,726 yards.

Ron Lancaster, who played for 19 seasons, was the most prolific passer in CFL history. Playing for Ottawa and Saskatchewan, Lancaster threw for 50,535 yards between 1960 and 1978. Lancaster also holds the CFL mark for career completions with 3,384 and attempts with 6,233. Not surprisingly, he is also the CFL record holder with an incredible 333 touchdown passes. By contrast, Fran Tarkenton is the NFL leader with 47,003 yards on 3,686 completions in 6,467 attempts and 342 touchdowns. Pretty close.

The record holder for the most passing yards in a single season is none other than Doug Flutie, who was a collegiate star at Boston College. Playing for British Columbia in 1991, Flutie threw for an amazing 6,619 yards. He did it by completing a record 466 passes. The NFL mark is 5,084 yards by Dan Marino. Warren Moon has the most completions with 404.

Doug Flutie

Saskatchewan quarterback Kent Austin set a CFL mark in 1992 by throwing the football 770 times. That broke Flutie's mark of 730 passes the year before. And neither of these guys had a sore arm. Moon holds the NFL mark with 655 attempts. But remember, Moon learned his craft in the CFL.

In 1966 Tom Clements, who preceded Joe Montana as the quarterback at Notre Dame, set a CFL mark for passing accuracy by completing 67.6 percent of his passes. Ken Anderson holds the NFL record with a 70.55 percentage.

Some of the CFL passing marks go back a long way. In 1954, Sam "the Rifle" Etcheverry of the Montreal Alouettes put on his passing shoes and threw for 586 yards in a single game. In 1991 the ever-

present Flutie came close to breaking it with a 582-yard performance. Norm Van Brocklin still holds the NFL mark with 554 yards gained.

On the receiving side, Terry Greer of Toronto set a record by catching 2,003 yards worth of passes in 1983. In the NFL, the season mark is held by Charley Hennigan with 1,746 yards.

Hal Patterson of Montreal set another long-standing record when he went deep all afternoon in 1956 and wound up with 338 yards on just 11 catches. Another amazing mark. Willie "Flipper" Anderson of the Los Angeles Rams set the NFL standard with 336 yards.

The all-time pass receiver is Rocky DiPietro of Hamilton, who grabbed 706 passes in a 14-year career. Art Monk of Washington had 888 through 1993 and was still active.

Brien Kelly of Edmonton is the leader in career yardage with 11,169 receiving yards in nine seasons. He grabbed 575 passes for an amazing 19.4 yards per catch and also set a CFL mark with 97 touchdown receptions. James Lofton had the NFL mark with 14,020 yards through 1993, while Jerry Rice of the 49ers had 118 TD receptions through 1993 and was still in his prime.

The single-season catching record is 118 receptions, set by Allen Pitts of Calgary in 1991. In the NFL, Sterling Sharpe of Green Bay broke his own record in 1993 with 112 catches.

No doubt that all these guys could really play the game. And notice how close most of the CFL and NFL marks are.

FAMOUS PLAYERS
WHO HAVE BEEN NORTH AND SOUTH

Not surprisingly, the players who have gained the most fame in the CFL are the quarterbacks. And because a good quarterback is always in demand, whenever a quarterback moved from the CFL to the NFL or from the National Football League to the Canadian Football League, he has been watched closely. Let's take a look at how some of the better-known signal-callers from each league have fared.

SAM ETCHEVERRY

Sam "the Rifle" Etcheverry is in the CFL Hall of Fame. He played nine seasons with the Montreal Alouettes, and threw for more than 25,000 yards with 183 touchdown passes in his final seven years, when official stats were kept. Etcheverry led the Eastern Division in passing for six straight years. But when he came south to the NFL St. Louis Cardinals in 1961, the Rifle didn't find the same success. He completed just 48.9 percent of his passes that year, was a part-timer the next year, then was gone, along with his former quarterbacking magic.

JOE KAPP

After an All-American career at the University of California, Joe Kapp went north to quarterback the British Columbia Lions. He became a CFL star, the best passer in the Western Division eight straight years from 1959 to 1966. In 1967 Kapp came south to the Minnesota Vikings, where he quickly became known as a tough, determined leader and winner, if not a picture-passer. Two years later he led the Vikes all the way to the Super Bowl. Injun Joe didn't have a long NFL career, but he proved he could do the job in either league.

TOBIN ROTE

Another successful quarterback was Tobin Rote, who led the Detroit Lions to an NFL championship in 1957. A few years later, Rote headed north and had several outstanding seasons with Toronto, leading the Eastern Division in passing from 1960 to 1962. A year later he was in the new American Football League and promptly led the San Diego Chargers to the 1963 AFL championship. No one can say Rote wasn't a winner, since he produced quality football in three different leagues.

JOE THEISMANN

Notre Dame All-American Joe Theismann opted for the CFL when some NFL scouts said he was too small and didn't have a strong enough arm. Theismann became a star with Toronto, throwing for 2,440 yards in 1971 and leading the Argonauts to the Grey Cup game. Two years later, in 1973, Joe again led the CFL East in passing yardage. The next season he headed south, joining the Washington Redskins, with whom he became an even bigger star. Theismann played for 12 years in Washington, eventually becoming an All-Pro and leading the Redskins to a Super Bowl championship.

DIETER BROCK

Dieter Brock was a longtime CFL quarterback who went south with high hopes. Playing 11 years for Winnipeg and Hamilton, Brock threw for 34,830 yards, third highest total in CFL history. In 1981 he threw for an impressive 4,796 yards. Then, in 1985, Brock signed with the Los Angeles Rams. Already in his mid-thirties, Brock produced a solid season, throwing for 2,658 yards with 16 TDs and only 13 interceptions. The Rams won their division and made it to the NFC title game before losing. But L.A. felt Brock just wasn't the man for the long haul and a year later turned to rookie Jim Everett. Brock never played in the NFL again. Maybe it was his age, or maybe the age-old notion that CFL-bred quarterbacks can't make the jump.

WARREN MOON

One quarterback who made it big was Warren Moon. When Moon came out of the University of Washington in 1977, he felt he wouldn't get a full shot in the NFL. So he went to Canada where he helped the Edmonton Eskimos win five straight Grey Cup championships. In 1983 Moon completed 380 of 664 passes for 5,648 yards. Then he came to Houston. Moon didn't lose a step. He soon became an NFL superstar, making the Oilers regular playoff contenders and being named the 1990 Offensive Player of the Year by the Associated Press. As of 1993 he had thrown for more than 51,000 yards in both leagues combined, the most in pro football history.

DOUG FLUTIE   That brings us to Doug Flutie. A great star at Boston College, Flutie threw for more than 10,500 yards from 1981 to 1984. Most NFL scouts felt that at 5'10" he was too short to be a pro star. But Flutie tried it for five years, drifting from one NFL team to another, looking for a full shot. He never got it. In 1990 he went to Canada. He was very good his first year as he got the feel of the game. Then, in 1991, he exploded with a record-setting performance. He completed 466 of 730 passes for 6,619 yards and 38 touchdowns. Moving to

Calgary in 1992, he continued to be a CFL superstar and is one of the biggest drawing cards and most exciting players the league has to offer.

"ROCKET" ISMAIL

A non-quarterback who created a great deal of excitement when he went north was all-purpose receiver-runner-returner Raghib "Rocket" Ismail, a Notre Dame consensus All-American in 1990. Ismail wasn't picked until the fourth round of the NFL draft, so this exciting performer went to Canada. Playing for Toronto, he was named the Eastern Division's Outstanding Rookie in 1991, catching 1,300 yards worth of passes and leading the league in combined yards with 2,959. In 1992 he set a CFL record for combined yards in one game with 401. Then in August 1993 Rocket Ismail signed a two-year contract to play for the Los Angeles Raiders, giving him a chance to become one of a handful of players to shine as superstars in both leagues.

Canadian football can be viewed on several United States cable channel outlets. With teams now playing in the United States, the league seems stronger than ever. Who knows, this wild, wide-open game with the large field may yet become a fan favorite south of the Canadian border. The CFL has produced great games and great players down through the years. For a true football fan, this brand of gridiron play is well worth watching.

14
College
Football
Facts and Figures

The Official NCAA Football Guide lists the participating colleges under several different classifications. There is Division I-A, Division I-AA, Division II, and Division III. All schedules are made within the divisions. In other words, a Division I-A school would not play a Division I-AA school, and a Division II school would not play a Division I (either A or AA) or a Division III school.

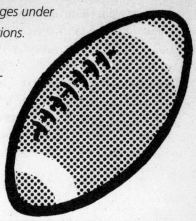

All schools in the above divisions are four-year colleges. When a school joins the NCAA, it can choose the division in which it wants to compete. And that means deciding just what kind of athletic program it can support.

The divisions have nothing to do with the size of the school in itself, but obviously, a smaller university cannot support a large-scale sports program. Division I schools must have at least seven different sports for men and seven sports for women. They can also have, for instance, six sports for men and eight for women or vice versa. There is also a limit to the number of scholarships permitted.

Division II and III schools must have at least four different sports for men and four for women. Division II schools offer a smaller number of scholarships than Division I. Division III schools offer no athletic scholarships whatsoever. Division I-A and I-AA are separated mainly by the size of the stadiums and the attendance at their games.

The majority of NFL players come from Division I-A schools. A fair number make it from Division I-AA. But it is rare for a player from Division II or III to make it in the pros. The best players usually go to Division I schools so they can play against the best on national television and before huge crowds.

THE HEISMAN TROPHY

Named after John Heisman, one of the great early college coaches in the game, the Heisman Trophy is given each year to the best college football player by the Downtown Athletic Club in New York City. The award was first given in 1935 and the winner was Jay Berwanger, a halfback out of the University of Chicago. In 1936 Berwanger was the NFL's top draft choice, picked by the Philadelphia Eagles.

Take a look at the list of Heisman winners. See how many names you recognize. Then compare it with the list of top NFL draft choices in Chapter 12. You'll see how many times the Heisman winner became a number-one draft pick.

Heisman Trophy Winners

Year	Player	Position	College
1935	Jay Berwanger	HB	Chicago
1936	Larry Kelley	E	Yale
1937	Clint Frank	HB	Yale
1938	Davey O'Brien	QB	Texas Christian
1939	Nile Kinnick	HB	Iowa
1940	Tom Harmon	HB	Michigan
1941	Bruce Smith	HB	Minnesota
1942	Frank Sinkwich	HB	Georgia
1943	Angelo Bertelli	QB	Notre Dame
1944	Les Horvath	QB	Ohio State
1945	Doc Blanchard	FB	Army
1946	Glenn Davis	HB	Army
1947	John Lujack	QB	Notre Dame
1948	Doak Walker	HB	Southern Methodist
1949	Leon Hart	E	Notre Dame
1950	Vic Janowicz	HB	Ohio State
1951	Dick Kazmaier	HB	Princeton

Heisman Trophy Winners

(continued)

Year	Player	Position	College
1952	Billy Vessels	HB	Oklahoma
1953	John Lattner	HB	Notre Dame
1954	Alan Ameche	FB	Wisconsin
1955	Howard Cassady	HB	Ohio State
1956	Paul Hornung	QB	Notre Dame
1957	John Crow	HB	Texas A&M
1958	Pete Dawkins	HB	Army
1959	Billy Cannon	HB	Louisiana State
1960	Joe Bellino	HB	Navy
1961	Ernie Davis	HB	Syracuse
1962	Terry Baker	QB	Oregon State
1963	Roger Staubach	QB	Navy
1964	John Huarte	QB	Notre Dame
1965	Mike Garrett	HB	Southern Cal (USC)
1966	Steve Spurrier	QB	Florida
1967	Gary Beban	QB	UCLA
1968	O. J. Simpson	HB	Southern Cal
1969	Steve Owens	HB	Oklahoma
1970	Jim Plunkett	QB	Stanford
1971	Pat Sullivan	QB	Auburn
1972	Johnny Rodgers	HB	Nebraska
1973	John Cappelletti	FB	Penn State
1974	Archie Griffin	HB	Ohio State
1975	Archie Griffin	HB	Ohio State
1976	Tony Dorsett	HB	Pittsburgh
1977	Earl Campbell	HB	Texas
1978	Billy Sims	HB	Oklahoma

Heisman Trophy Winners
(continued)

Year	Player	Position	College
1979	Charles White	HB	Southern Cal
1980	George Rogers	HB	South Carolina
1981	Marcus Allen	HB	Southern Cal
1982	Herschel Walker	HB	Georgia
1983	Mike Rozier	HB	Nebraska
1984	Doug Flutie	QB	Boston College
1985	Bo Jackson	HB	Auburn
1986	Vinny Testaverde	QB	Miami
1987	Tim Brown	WR	Notre Dame
1988	Barry Sanders	HB	Oklahoma State
1989	Andre Ware	QB	Houston
1990	Ty Detmer	QB	Brigham Young
1991	Desmond Howard	WR	Michigan
1992	Gino Torretta	QB	Miami
1993	Charlie Ward	QB	Florida State

Remember how many top NFL draft choices were quarterbacks or running backs? The Heisman Trophy has shown even more preference for those glamour players. Except for a handful of pass receivers, all the award winners have been quarterbacks or running backs. No lineman or linebacker has ever won, nor has a defensive back. It's always the high-profile player.

And how many Heisman winners became the NFL's number-one choice? The answer is 16. Remember, Heisman winners from Army and Navy couldn't be chosen because they had to go into the service. That eliminates Blanchard, Glenn Davis, Dawkins, Bellino, and Staubach. Of those, Davis eventually played some pro ball, Bellino tried but didn't make it, and Staubach became a superstar and Hall of Famer.

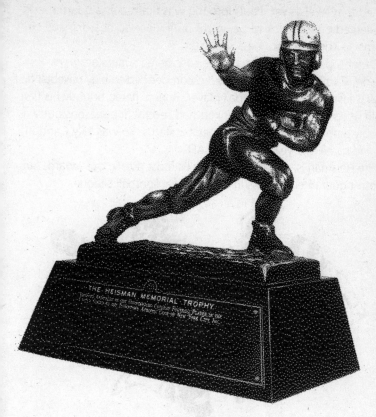

The Heisman Trophy

How about the 16 who became top choices? They were Berwanger, Harmon, Sinkwich, Bertelli, Hart, Hornung, Cannon, Ernie Davis, Baker, Simpson, Plunkett, Campbell, Sims, Rogers, Jackson, and Testaverde. Most of them became fine pros. But there were some exceptions.

Ernie Davis never had a chance. Drafted by Washington, then traded to Cleveland so he could play alongside another Syracuse alumnus, Jim Brown, in a dream backfield, Davis fell ill during his first training camp. He was diagnosed with leukemia and died tragically before he could play a pro game.

Terry Baker had difficulty adjusting to the pro game and eventually left. Vinny Testaverde was expected to be a superstar but hasn't reached that level as yet. Paul Hornung was drafted as a quarterback and seemed on the brink of being cut until Vince Lombardi made him a halfback. Then he became a superstar.

Other top choices who could be considered superstars were Simpson, Campbell, and Sims. Bo Jackson decided to play baseball first and was just a part-time football player. Rogers flared brightly his first couple of years, then faded. Plunkett had several fine seasons but was probably a notch or two below superstar status. So was Billy Cannon, who had some fine years in the old AFL.

The Heisman is still college football's most prestigious award. But it doesn't guarantee success in the National Football League.

NATIONAL CHAMPIONS

The collegiate national champion has been selected by a number of different organizations over the years, including the Helms Athletic Foundation, the Dickinson System, the Football Writers Association of America, the Associated Press, United Press International, and, most recently, USA Today/CNN. Here is a list of national champions from 1936 to 1993, their record, and the team's coach. If the voting bodies disagreed, all winners are listed.

The records are for the regular season. Up to 1950 the winner was picked before bowl games. After 1950 the bowl games were taken into consideration. The "W" or "L" after the record indicates whether the national champ won or lost its bowl game. (Note: Some of the teams selected did not compete in a bowl game.)

See how many times your favorite team has been a national champ.

National Champions

Year	Team	Record	Coach
1936	Minnesota	7-1-0	Bernie Bierman
1937	Pittsburgh	9-0-1	Jock Sutherland
1938	Texas Christian	10-0-0 W	Leo "Dutch" Meyer
1939	Texas A&M	10-0-0 W	Homer Norton
1940	Minnesota	8-0-0	Bernie Bierman
1941	Minnesota	8-0-0	Bernie Bierman
1942	Ohio State	9-1-0	Paul Brown
1943	Notre Dame	9-1-0	Frank Leahy
1944	Army	9-0-0	Earl "Red" Blaik
1945	Army	9-0-0	Earl "Red" Blaik
1946	Notre Dame	8-0-1	Frank Leahy
1947	Notre Dame	9-0-0	Frank Leahy
1948	Michigan	9-0-0	Bennie Oosterbaan
1949	Notre Dame	10-0-0	Frank Leahy
1950	Oklahoma	10-0-0	Bud Wilkinson
1951	Tennessee	10-0-0 L	Bob Neyland
1952	Michigan State	9-0-0	Biggie Munn
1953	Maryland	10-0-0 L	Jim Tatum
1954	UCLA	9-0-0	Red Sanders
	Ohio State	9-0-0 W	Woody Hayes
1955	Oklahoma	10-0-0 W	Bud Wilkinson

National Champions

(continued)

Year	Team	Record	Coach
1956	Oklahoma	10-0-0	Bud Wilkinson
1957	Ohio State	8-1-0 W	Woody Hayes
	Auburn	10-0-0	Ralph "Shug" Jordan
1958	Louisiana State	10-0-0 W	Paul Dietzel
	Iowa	7-1-1 W	Forest Evashevski
1959	Syracuse	10-0-0 W	Ben Schwartzwalder
1960	Minnesota	8-1-0 L	Murray Warmath
	Mississippi	9-0-1 W	John Vaught
1961	Alabama	10-0-0 W	Paul "Bear" Bryant
	Ohio State	8-0-1	Woody Hayes
1962	Southern Cal	10-0-0 W	John McKay
1963	Texas	10-0-0 W	Darrell Royal
1964	Alabama	10-0-0 L	Paul "Bear" Bryant
	Arkansas	10-0-0 L	Frank Broyles
	Notre Dame	9-1-0	Ara Parseghian
1965	Alabama	8-1-1 W	Paul "Bear" Bryant
	Michigan State	10-0-0 L	Duffy Daugherty
1966	Notre Dame	9-0-1	Ara Parseghian
	Michigan State	9-0-1	Duffy Daugherty
1967	Southern Cal	9-1-0 W	John McKay
1968	Ohio State	9-0-0 W	Woody Hayes
1969	Texas	10-0-0 W	Darrell Royal
1970	Nebraska	10-0-1 W	Bob Devaney
	Texas	10-0-0 L	Darrell Royal
	Ohio State	9-0-0 L	Woody Hayes
1971	Nebraska	12-0-0 W	Bob Devaney
1972	Southern Cal	11-0-0 W	John McKay
1973	Notre Dame	10-0-0	Ara Parseghian
	Alabama	11-0-0 L	Paul "Bear" Bryant

National Champions
(continued)

Year	Team	Record	Coach
1974	Southern Cal	9-1-1 W	John McKay
	Oklahoma	11-0-0	Barry Switzer
1975	Oklahoma	10-1-0 W	Barry Switzer
1976	Pittsburgh	11-1-0 W	Johnny Majors
1977	Notre Dame	10-1-0 W	Dan Devine
1978	Alabama	10-1-0 W	Paul "Bear" Bryant
	Southern Cal	11-1-0 W	John Robinson
1979	Alabama	11-0-0 W	Paul "Bear" Bryant
1980	Georgia	11-0-0 W	Vince Dooley
1981	Clemson	11-0-0 W	Danny Ford
1982	Penn State	10-1-0 W	Joe Paterno
1983	Miami (Fla.)	10-1-0 W	Howard Schnellenberger
1984	Brigham Young	12-0-0 W	LaVell Edwards
1985	Oklahoma	10-1-0 W	Barry Switzer
1986	Penn State	11-0-0 W	Joe Paterno
1987	Miami (Fla.)	11-0-0 W	Jimmy Johnson
1988	Notre Dame	11-0-0 W	Lou Holtz
1989	Miami (Fla.)	10-1-0 W	Dennis Erickson
1990	Colorado	11-1-1 W	Bill McCartney
	Georgia Tech	11-0-1 W	Bobby Ross
1991	Washington	12-0-0 W	Don James
	Miami (Fla.)	12-0-0 W	Dennis Erickson
1992	Alabama	12-0-0 W	Gene Stallings
1993	Florida State	11-1-0 W	Bobby Bowden

THE BOWL GAMES

Some of the biggest highlights in college football are the post season bowl games. They provide chances for many of the best teams in the land to play each other before huge crowds and on national television. There are also spectacular halftime shows and a great deal of pomp and pageantry.

The Rose Bowl, called the "granddaddy of them all," was first played in 1902. The game was then stopped until 1916, but has been played every New Year's Day since. Most college teams are grouped into conferences, which are organized according to the schools' location and academic standing. Since 1947 the Rose Bowl game has featured the winner of the Pacific Ten (Pac-Ten; formerly the Pac-Eight) conference against the top team in the Big Ten conference. The Rose Bowl is located in Pasadena, California, and has a seating capacity of 104,000. The stadium is often packed for the big New Year's Day game.

Until the mid-1930s the Rose Bowl stood alone as college football's post season spectacle. Then in 1935 both the Orange Bowl and the Sugar Bowl began, followed by the Cotton Bowl in 1937. These have always been the big four bowl games. The Gator Bowl, begun in 1946, is often looked upon as a fifth major bowl.

The Orange Bowl is located in Miami, Florida, and has a capacity of

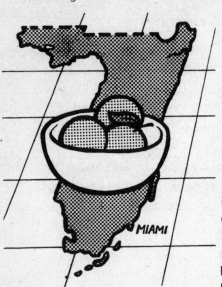

74,244. The Sugar Bowl is in New Orleans, Louisiana, and seats 72,704, while the Cotton Bowl is located in Dallas, Texas, and plays to a full house of 72,032 fans. Renovation of the Gator Bowl in Jacksonville, Florida, will reduce seating from 80,129 to 73,000.

Other postseason bowl games include the John Hancock Bowl (formerly the Sun Bowl) in El Paso, Texas; the Florida Citrus Bowl (formerly the Tangerine Bowl), in Orlando, Florida; the Liberty Bowl in Memphis,

Tennessee; the Peach Bowl in Atlanta, Georgia; the Fiesta Bowl in Tempe, Arizona; the Independence Bowl in Shreveport, Louisiana; the Holiday Bowl in San Diego, California; the California Bowl in Fresno, California; the Aloha Bowl in Honolulu, Hawaii; the Freedom Bowl in Anaheim, California; the Hall of Fame Bowl in Tampa, Florida; the Copper Bowl in Tucson, Arizona; and the Blockbuster Bowl in Miami, Florida.

THE BOWL GAMES AND THE NATIONAL CHAMPIONSHIP

In recent years, college football has been looking for a better way to choose its national champion. Some have proposed a tournament such as the NCAA basketball tournament in which the winner is declared national champion. But this is not practical in football where teams play just once a week.

In 1992 the various bowl committees got together to work out a formula in which there was a good chance that the top two teams in the country would face each other in one of the bowl games, making the winner of that game the unofficial national champion.

As mentioned earlier, the Rose Bowl is still limited to the Big Ten winner versus the Pac-Ten winner. Let's look at the other major bowls. The Orange Bowl features the top team in the Big Eight Conference against a team to be chosen. The Sugar Bowl pits the Southeastern Conference winner against a team to be picked by the bowl committee. The Cotton Bowl has the winner in the Southwest Athletic Conference going against a team to be chosen. It is hoped that from among the group one of the games will be for the national title.

It worked out that at the end of the 1993 season one of the games was for the national title. In the Orange Bowl, the Florida State Seminoles of the Atlantic Coast Conference met the Nebraska Cornhuskers of the Big Eight. They were the top two teams in the polls, and when the smoke cleared, Florida State had an 18-16 victory and a national title. The system still isn't perfect, but it's the best available for now.

SOME BOWL GAME FACTS AND RECORDS

By defeating Nebraska, 18-16, in the Orange Bowl game following the 1993 season, Florida State tied a record by winning a bowl game for the ninth consecutive season.

The University of Southern California (USC) shares the record for the most consecutive bowl-game victories with nine. The Trojans' streak ran from 1923 to 1945, with eight of the victories coming in the Rose Bowl and the other in the 1924 Los Angeles Christmas Festival game.

Not surprisingly, Alabama's Paul "Bear" Bryant coached the most bowl victories with 15. In fact, the Crimson Tide has won more bowl games than any other team, having chalked up 25 bowl victories through the 1992 season. USC has the second most bowl victories with 22, followed by the University of Oklahoma with 19.

On January 1, 1993, the University of Washington just missed becoming the first team to win three consecutive Rose Bowls. After beating Iowa and Michigan the two previous years, the Huskies were beaten by Michigan in a rematch, 38-31.

A few of the major schools that have not fared well in bowl games include Arkansas (9-15-3), Brigham Young (5-11-1), Colorado (6-11), Louisiana State (11-16), Texas Christian (4-9), and perhaps the most luckless bowl team of them all, the University of South Carolina. The Gamecocks have gone to bowl games eight times … and have lost them all!

Here are the results of the five major bowls from 1980 to the present, showing how your favorite teams have done over the past few years. The 1980 scores are for the 1979 season and so on, since all bowls except the Gator are played on New Year's Day. The Gator is usually played toward the end of December, although occasionally the game has taken place on January 1 or 2.

Rose Bowl

Year	Winner	Score	Loser	Score
1980	Southern Cal	17	Ohio State	16
1981	Michigan	23	Washington	6
1982	Washington	28	Iowa	0
1983	UCLA	24	Michigan	14
1984	UCLA	45	Illinois	9
1985	Southern Cal	20	Ohio State	17
1986	UCLA	45	Iowa	28
1987	Arizona State	22	Michigan	15
1988	Michigan State	20	Southern Cal	17
1989	Michigan	22	Southern Cal	14
1990	Southern Cal	17	Michigan	10
1991	Washington	46	Iowa	34
1992	Washington	34	Michigan	14
1993	Michigan	38	Washington	31
1994	Wisconsin	21	UCLA	16

Orange Bowl

Year	Winner	Score	Loser	Score
1980	Oklahoma	24	Florida State	7
1981	Oklahoma	18	Florida State	17
1982	Clemson	22	Nebraska	15
1983	Nebraska	21	Louisiana State	20
1984	Miami (Fla.)	31	Nebraska	30
1985	Washington	28	Oklahoma	17
1986	Oklahoma	25	Penn State	10
1987	Oklahoma	42	Arkansas	8
1988	Miami (Fla.)	20	Oklahoma	14
1989	Miami (Fla.)	23	Nebraska	3
1990	Notre Dame	21	Colorado	6
1991	Colorado	10	Notre Dame	9
1992	Miami (Fla.)	22	Nebraska	0
1993	Florida State	27	Nebraska	14
1994	Florida State	18	Nebraska	16

Cotton Bowl

1980	Houston	17	Nebraska	14
1981	Alabama	30	Baylor	2
1982	Texas	14	Alabama	12
1983	Southern Methodist	7	Pittsburgh	3
1984	Georgia	10	Texas	9
1985	Boston College	45	Houston	28
1986	Texas A&M	36	Auburn	16
1987	Ohio State	28	Texas A&M	12
1988	Texas A&M	35	Notre Dame	10
1989	UCLA	17	Arkansas	3
1990	Tennessee	31	Arkansas	27
1991	Miami (Fla.)	46	Texas	3
1992	Florida State	10	Texas A&M	2
1993	Notre Dame	28	Texas A&M	3
1994	Notre Dame	24	Texas A&M	21

Sugar Bowl

1980	Alabama	24	Arkansas	9
1981	Georgia	17	Notre Dame	10
1982	Pittsburgh	24	Georgia	20
1983	Penn State	27	Georgia	23
1984	Auburn	9	Michigan	7
1985	Nebraska	28	Louisiana State	10
1986	Tennessee	35	Miami (Fla.)	7
1987	Nebraska	30	Louisiana State	15
1988	Syracuse	16	Auburn	16
1989	Florida State	13	Auburn	7
1990	Miami (Fla.)	33	Alabama	25
1991	Tennessee	23	Virginia	22
1992	Notre Dame	39	Florida	28
1993	Alabama	34	Miami (Fla.)	13
1994	Florida	41	West Virginia	7

Gator Bowl

Year	Winner	Score	Loser	Score
1980	North Carolina	17	Michigan	15
1981	Pittsburgh	37	South Carolina	9
1982	North Carolina	31	Arkansas	27
1983	Florida State	31	West Virginia	12
1984	Florida	14	Iowa	6
1985	Oklahoma State	21	South Carolina	14
1986	Florida State	34	Oklahoma State	23
1987	Clemson	27	Stanford	21
1988	Louisiana State	30	South Carolina	13
1989	Georgia	34	Michigan State	27
1990	Clemson	27	West Virginia	7
1991	Michigan	35	Mississippi	3
1992	Oklahoma	48	Virginia	14
1993	Florida	27	North Carolina State	10
1994	Alabama	24	North Carolina State	10

RECORDS AND ACHIEVEMENTS

Here is a brief look at some of the great individual records in the college game. Once again football fans will recognize many of the names, especially those players who went on to great careers in the NFL.

Ty Detmer. Quarterbacking the Brigham Young Cougars from 1988 to 1991, Detmer set a collegiate record by generating 14,665 yards of total offense, an incredible 318.8 yards a game for his college career.

David Klingler. When it comes to total offense in a single season, no one comes close to Houston's David Klingler. Playing in 11 games in 1990, Klingler ran 704 plays for 5,221 yards, an average of 474.6 yards per game. Amazing.

Ty Detmer. For just pure passing, Detmer is again tops. From 1988 to 1991, he completed 958 passes in 1,530 attempts for 15,031 yards and 121 touchdowns. All those numbers are national records.

Jim McMahon. Here's a surprise. When he was at Brigham Young back in 1980, McMahon compiled the highest quarterback rating for a single season. He completed 284 passes in 445 tries for 4,571 yards and 47 touchdowns. His rating of 176.9 is still a record, even though passing has become more common since McMahon left the college game.

David Klingler. Klingler, again. In 1990 he set an NCAA single-season mark with 54 touchdown passes. He also averaged 467.3 passing yards a game and on one glorious day threw for an incredible total of 716 yards. That's passing for you.

Ed Marinaro. This one goes back to 1969-1971. Ed Marinaro, who would become a popular television actor (Hill Street Blues), was the tailback at Cornell. In 27 games he rushed for 4,715 yards, a record average of 174.6 yards per game. Listen to the three names behind Marinaro: O.J. Simpson, Herschel Walker, Tony Dorsett. Marinaro topped them all.

Barry Sanders. In 1988, Barry Sanders of Oklahoma State blew away all the single-season rushing marks. The future Detroit Lions All-Pro ran the ball 344 times in 11 games for a record 2,628 yards, a record 37 touchdowns, and a record 232.1 yards per game. He broke the old mark set by Marcus Allen of USC in 1981.

Tony Dorsett. The best four-year rushing mark in college history still belongs to Tony Dorsett. A star from his freshman year on, Touchdown Tony ran the ball 1,074 times between 1973 and 1976 and gained 6,082 yards, an average of 5.66 yards per carry.

Manny Hazard. Playing for the University of Houston in 1989, Manny Hazard grabbed a record 142 passes in 11 games, setting yet another mark with 22 touchdown catches. His quarterback that year was Heisman Trophy-winner Andre Ware.

Aaron Turner. It is Aaron Turner of Pacific (Cal.) who holds the career record for catches and total receiving yards. Playing from 1989 to 1992, Turner caught 266 passes for 4,345 yards.

Barry Sanders. Running for Oklahoma State in 1988, Sanders set a new record by scoring 39 touchdowns and 234 points. That's an average of 21.3 points a game, still another record.

Anthony Thompson. Thompson, who played running back at Indiana from 1986 to 1989, holds the career record with 65 touchdowns and 394 points. Four of those points came on conversions.

Reggie Roby. Known as an All-Pro punter with the Miami Dolphins in the 1980s, Reggie Roby also made his mark kicking at Iowa. From 1979 to 1982, he set a collegiate record by averaging 45.6 yards on 172 punts.

Napoleon McCallum. A halfback at the United States Naval Academy from 1981 to 1985, McCallum set a record for all-purpose yards that still stands. In four years he rushed for 4,179 yards, caught 796 yards worth of passes, took back punts for another 858 yards and returned kickoffs to the tune of 1,339 yards. That's a total of 7,172 yards, quite an impressive workload for anyone.

COLLEGE RUSHING CHAMPS

Here's a list of just some of the stars who have won a college rushing championship since the first one was taken in 1937 by Byron "Whizzer" White. Some of the other top runners were Ollie Matson, Dick Bass, Brian Piccolo, Mike Garrett, O. J. Simpson, Ed Marinaro, Ricky Bell, Tony Dorsett, Earl Campbell, Billy Sims, Charles White, George Rogers, Marcus Allen, Keith Byers, Barry Sanders, and Marshall Faulk. Most of those names will sound very familiar to pro football fans. Once a running star, always a running star. Almost.

RECORDS SET AT SMALL COLLEGES

Neil Lomax. Lomax, who would go on to a fine career in the NFL, set a Division I-AA record back in 1979 while playing for Portland State. He put the ball in the air an amazing 77 times for a new mark in a game against Northern Colorado. Lomax also holds the career records for completions with 938 and attempts with 1,606.

Jerry Rice. This is the man many consider the greatest pass receiver ever because of his play with the San Francisco 49ers. Rice went to Mississippi Valley, a Division I-AA school, and did he ever set records! Listen to a few. He holds the mark for passes caught in a game (24) and a career (301). He is also the record holder for most yards gained receiving in a season (1,682) and career (4,693). He caught passes for 100 yards or more in 23 games, and set records with 27 touchdown catches in a season and 50 for his career. He also set records for catching touchdown passes in 10 different games during a season and 26 games during his career, and for grabbing a TD toss in 17

straight contests. Sounds like he came into the pros without missing a beat.

Johnny Bailey. Not very many Division II players make it to the NFL. Johnny Bailey of Texas A&I is one who did, and he holds most of the Division II rushing records. In four years Bailey ran for 6,320 yards, including an amazing 2,011 as a freshman in 1986.

Heath Sherman. He was Johnny Bailey's running mate at Texas A&I for three years. In 1986 the two combined with 3,526 yards, a record for a duo, with Sherman adding 1,515 to Bailey's 2,011. Sherman also made it to the pros and had an outstanding year with the Philadelphia Eagles in 1992.

Willie Totten. Totten was the Mississippi Valley quarterback who had the pleasure of throwing to Jerry Rice, among others. From 1982 to 1985, Totten generated 13,007 yards in total offense, an all-division collegiate record of 325.2 yards per game.

THE BEST TEAMS

Here are the 20 most successful college football teams over the years. They are ranked not by the total number of victories, but rather by won-lost percentage. The records are through the 1993 season. The records include Bowl Games.

The Best Teams

Team	Yrs.	Won	Lost	Tied	Pct.
1. Notre Dame	105	723	211	41	.763
2. Michigan	114	739	242	36	.744
3. Alabama	99	691	237	44	.733
4. Oklahoma	99	659	240	52	.720
5. Texas	101	687	273	32	.709
6. Ohio State	104	659	265	53	.702
7. Southern Cal	101	630	254	52	.701
8. Penn State	107	674	291	41	.691
8. Nebraska	104	673	290	40	.691
10. Tennessee	97	636	276	53	.687
11. Central Mich.	93	480	255	36	.646
12. Florida State	47	316	176	16	.638
13. Washington	104	562	310	49	.637
14. Army	104	588	327	50	.635
15. Miami (Ohio)	105	546	308	42	.633
16. Georgia	100	589	333	53	.632
17. Louisiana State	100	573	325	46	.631
17. Arizona State	81	444	255	24	.631
19. Auburn	101	558	330	46	.622
20. Colorado	104	557	348	36	.611

Longest Winning Streaks

Team	Wins	Years
Oklahoma	47	1953 - 1957
Washington	39	1908 - 1914
Yale	37	1890 - 1893
Yale	37	1887 - 1889
Toledo	35	1969 - 1971
Pennsylvania	34	1894 - 1896
Oklahoma	31	1948 - 1950
Pittsburgh	31	1914 - 1918
Pennsylvania	31	1896 - 1898
Texas	30	1968 - 1970

THE TOP COACHES

No one can say who is the "best" college—or the best NFL—coach. But there are coaches whose long-term success speaks for itself. There are also coaches who have become well-known sports personalities in their own right. Here is a list of the best and most recognizable coaches in the college game and their records over the years. They are listed by winning percentage.

The records of active coaches run through 1993 and include all bowl games. Records are the total for all schools at which the person coached.

Top College Coaches

Coach	School(s)	Years	Won	Lost	Tied	Pct.
Knute Rockne	Notre Dame	13	105	12	5	.881
Frank Leahy	Notre Dame	11	107	13	9	.864
	Boston College	2				
Barry Switzer	Oklahoma	16	157	29	4	.837
Bud Wilkinson	Oklahoma	17	145	29	4	.826
Tom Osborne*	Nebraska	19	206	47	3	.811
Bob Devaney	Nebraska	16	136	30	7	.806
Joe Paterno*	Penn State	26	257	69	3	.786
"Bear" Bryant	Alabama	25	323	85	17	.780
	Kentucky	8				
	Texas A&M	4				
	Maryland	1				
Bo Schembechler	Michigan	21	234	65	8	.775
	Miami (Ohio)	6				
Red Blaik	Army	18	166	48	14	.759
	Dartmouth	7				
Bobby Bowden*	Florida State	18	239	78	3	.752
	West Virginia	6				
	Samford	4				

Top College Coaches
(continued)

Coach	School(s)	Years	Won	Lost	Tied	Pct.
Darrell Royal	Texas	19	184	60	5	.749
	Mississippi State	3				
	Washington	1				
John McKay	Southern Cal	16	127	40	8	.749
Ara Parseghian	Notre Dame	11	170	58	6	.739
	Northwestern	8				
	Miami (Ohio)	5				
Glenn "Pop" Warner	Carlisle and many others	44	313	106	32	.729
Eddie Robinson*	Grambling	51	388	140	15	.728
LaVell Edwards*	Brigham Young	22	197	73	3	.727

* Denotes active coach

15

The **Wild** and **Wacky**
World of
College Football

College football has been around a long time. There are teams located all around the United States, and hundreds of games are played every weekend during the season. Not surprisingly, the college gridiron has produced more than its share of unusual happenings — strange, funny, and unexpected things that have become part of football lore. Let's take a look at some of them.

THE TACKLE FROM NOWHERE

It was Alabama against Rice in the Cotton Bowl on January 1, 1954. Alabama's Crimson Tide was led by quarterback Bart Starr, who would go on to NFL fame with the Green Bay Packers. The Rice attack was spearheaded by an All-American halfback named Dickie Moegle. Early in the second period Moegle broke loose for a 79-yard touchdown run that tied the game. The extra point gave Rice a 7-6 lead.

Minutes later Rice recovered an Alabama fumble and took over at the Rice five. Sure enough, Moegle got the call and took off down the right sideline. It looked to everyone present that the speedy star was about to run 95 yards for another touchdown. But just after Moegle crossed the midfield line, it happened. Without warning, a helmetless player who was standing in front of the Alabama bench leaped onto the field and tackled the startled Moegle. The refs had no choice but to award Moegle a 95-yard touchdown, since no one who was actually in the game at the time could have caught him. Rice won the game, 28-6.

The player who had tackled Moegle was Alabama fullback Tommy Lewis, who had scored a touchdown early in the game. Asked why he bolted off the bench to make an illegal stop, an embarrassed Lewis could only say:

"I guess I was too full of Alabama."

WRONG-WAY RIEGELS

Another bowl game witnessed one of the strangest plays ever seen on the gridiron. It happened at the Rose Bowl on January 1, 1929. The University of California was meeting Georgia Tech. In the second period Tech had the ball and was starting to move upfield. Then there was a fumble, the ball squirting loose at the Georgia Tech 35. Several players from each team began converging on it.

Cal defensive back Roy Riegels got there first and scooped the ball up. He moved toward the Tech goal, then bumped into a tackler and spun around. When he took off again he was… running the wrong way! Riegels had somehow become confused and was now headed full speed toward his own goal line.

The only man chasing him was a teammate, Benny Lom. Believe it or not, Lom tackled Riegels on the one-yard line. When Riegels saw what had happened he tried to get up, but was buried by several Georgia Tech players. Cal then tried to punt, only to have the kick blocked into the end zone for a Tech safety. Those two points would provide the margin of victory in an 8-7 Georgia Tech win.

Riegels always blamed himself, saying, "When I pivoted to get away from that tackler I completely lost my bearings."

But as "Wrong Way-Riegels" he found his way into football legend.

THE ALL-TIME LAUGHER

A one-sided game is often called a laugher. That's because the team that is in the lead is so far ahead that its players can laugh and enjoy themselves. There's no real chance of losing. Well, the ultimate laugher came on October 7, 1916, when mighty Georgia Tech hosted tiny Cumberland College in Atlanta. Oddly enough, Cumberland had been a powerful team in the early 1900s. But by 1916 they were playing on an informal basis.

As soon as the game started it was obvious that Tech was a much superior team. But what happened after that is almost impossible to believe, even today. Tech just started running through Cumberland and scoring touchdowns. One, two, three, four… Every time the Tech players got the ball they scored. By the end of the first quarter it was already 63-0. A laugher. Well, get this. At halftime the score was 126-0.

The onslaught continued. It was 180-0 after three, and at the end of the second half—mercifully shortened by 15 minutes—Tech was in front 222-0! It was the most one-sided game in football history. Tech scored on all 32 possessions. They gained 501 yards on the ground, scored on five of six interceptions, five of nine punt returns, two of three fumble recovery returns, and one kickoff return. Cumberland's net offense was minus 42 yards.

Perhaps, however, the most outrageous thing to happen was the statement made after the game by Cumberland's Charlie Warwick.

"We were sort of getting to 'em in that last quarter," he said.

He was kidding, wasn't he?

ONE AMAZING COMEBACK

Whenever Notre Dame met the University of Southern California in the 1960s and 1970s it was a war. The two teams had become bitter rivals and often spoilers of each other's fortunes. Their annual late-season game was anxiously awaited by fans all over the country. When Ara Parseghian's Notre Dame team rolled into California in 1974 it was the number one defensive team in the country, having yielded just nine touchdowns in 10 previous games.

The defense clicked as usual, but so did the offense. With just minutes left in the first half, Notre Dame's Fighting Irish held a 24-0 lead. And with that great defense, it looked as if USC's Trojans were finished. But then as time ran down in the half, USC quarterback Pat

Haden hit tailback Anthony Davis with a short touchdown toss. The extra point was missed, but it was now a 24-6 game. It was the second half, though, that really stunned everyone.

It started when Davis made a brilliant, 100-yard return of the opening kickoff. Minutes later A.D., as he was called, scored again. The kick made it 24-19. After the Irish fumbled, USC marched again and Davis scored from the four. He also ran in a two-point conversion to give USC a 27-24 lead. But the Trojans didn't stop there.

Two more third-period scores gave USC a 41-24 lead. In the fourth period, USC continued to move the ball and took it into the end zone twice more. The final was 55-24, a shocking score by itself. But the fact that Southern Cal had scored 55 unanswered points in just 17 minutes against the number-one defense in the country had everyone buzzing. Anthony Davis and the Trojans were unstoppable.

DUKE FOR THE DEFENSE

Talk about putting all your eggs in one basket. The 1938 Duke Blue Devils seemed to do just that. The basket was defense. The Blue Devils were just incredible when defending their goal line. On the other hand, when they went on offense, well, they looked like an inept sandlot team.

But the defense kept winning for them. It was so good that not one opponent could score a single point against the team in the regular season. Duke finished at 9-0. In five of the nine games, the offense scored seven or fewer points, but with a perfect defense, it was enough. Then on January 2, 1939, Duke traveled to Pasadena to meet the University of Southern California in the Rose Bowl. Would defense win for them again?

Sure enough, Duke took a 3-0 lead into the closing minutes. USC had the ball at the Blue Devil 34. That's when the Trojans put a fourth-string quarterback named Doyle Nave into the game. Out of nowhere, Nave hit on three straight passes to back-up receiver Al Krueger. Then, with 41 seconds left, Nave spotted Krueger in the end zone and fired a pass for the winning touchdown.

USC in winning the game, 7-3, had done what no other team during the entire season could do. The Duke defense had held its opponents scoreless for 599 minutes and 19 seconds of a 600-minute season. It was the final 41 seconds that cost the Blue Devils an unbeaten season and a Rose Bowl triumph.

AND THE BAND PLAYED ON

This one is still hard to believe. It's something that couldn't happen. But it did, and no one who saw it will ever forget. The game was between Stanford University with its All-American quarterback John Elway, and the University of California. It took place at Memorial Stadium in Berkeley on November 20, 1982. And until the final four seconds, it was simply an exciting, competitive football game.

California had a 19-17 lead as Elway drove his team downfield in the final minutes. With just four seconds left, Stanford's Mark Harmon came on and booted a clutch, 35-yard field goal to give his team a

20-19 lead and an apparent victory. California would have time to run back the kickoff, but that was all.

Because of a penalty, Stanford kicked off from its own 25. Cal's Kevin Moen took it at the 43 and started upfield. He ran toward the left sideline as several Stanford tacklers took aim. Suddenly, he lateraled the ball to teammate Richard Rodgers, who was running behind him. Rodgers grabbed the pigskin and sprinted past midfield. Just when he was about to be hit he lateraled the ball to Dwight Garner at the Stanford 44. Garner took several steps and was hit. But before he went down he managed to lateral back to Rodgers, who was at the 48.

Rodgers cut toward the middle of the field and then lateraled back to Mariet Ford at the 46. It looked like a game of football, football, who's got the football. Miraculously, Ford found running room and began sprinting toward the goal line. The Stanford band was already gathering near the goal line ready for the anticipated victory celebration.

At the 25 Ford was trapped. Without looking, he tossed a blind lateral over his right shoulder. Suddenly, Kevin Moen had it again. He was the guy who started the whole play. As Moen ran toward the goal line he began cutting around the Stanford band members who were on the field. They actually were blocking out their team's tacklers. There was near pandemonium as Moen crossed the goal line, knocking over a trombone player who was in his way.

Confusion reigned. Then, the referee put his hands in the air to signal a touchdown. The crowd went wild. Stanford protested, but the TD counted. There had been five legal laterals during the 57-yard touchdown run, which took a lot longer than four seconds. But the rules allowed for the play to be completed.

In one of the strangest finishes to a football game ever, California had won, 25-20, thanks to some crazy laterals, some luck, and their opponents' band preparing for a victory song.

HARVARD "BEATS" YALE, 29-29

No, that headline is not a misprint. It actually appeared in the Harvard Crimson, the school newspaper, after the two universities met in an epic battle on November 23, 1968. Both came in with identical 8-0 records, so not only was an unbeaten season at stake, the Ivy League championship stood in the balance as well.

For most of the game Yale dominated. With just 3:31 left in the game, the Elis held a comfortable 29-13 lead. Harvard had the ball, but way back on its own 14-yard line. With reserve quarterback Frank Champi in the game, the Crimson began to march. They drove downfield, but by the time they reached the Yale 15, there were just 42 seconds left. Then Champi hit Bruce Freeman with a pass at the three, and Freeman carried it in for the score. A two-point conversion made it 29-21. But time was running out.

Harvard tried an onside kick. There was a skirmish for the ball and the Crimson's Bill Kelly had it at the Yale 49. Champi scrambled for 14 yards and a 15-yard penalty brought the ball to the 20 with 20 seconds left. Fullback Gus Crim ran for 14 to the six, but then Champi was thrown for a two-yard loss back to the eight.

With four seconds left, Champi took the snap and moved out of the pocket. With several Yale defenders chasing him he threw on the run and hit Vic Gatto in the end zone for the score. There was no time left on the clock, but Harvard had one more play: a shot at the conversion.

Champi then dropped back and calmly hit Pete Varney in the end zone for the two points and the 29-29 deadlock. The place went wild. Champi had brought his team back from a 22-0 deficit and the brink of oblivion at 29-13. No wonder the paper said "Harvard Beats Yale, 29-29." That kind of finish is as good as a win.

WHO WAS THAT GUY?

One of college football's unsolved mysteries unfolded on November 23, 1935, the day that Princeton and Dartmouth were to meet in a battle of unbeaten Ivy League teams. The game was played at Palmer Stadium in Princeton on a cold and snowy afternoon.

The field was wet, muddy, and very slippery. Dartmouth's shoes couldn't be fitted with the standard mud cleat and, as one Dartmouth player said, "It was like play-ing on grease."

The Princeton Tigers had a 13-6 lead at the half, and after intermission they began to build on it. Another score made it 20-6. With the snow turning to sleet, Princeton drove again late in the fourth quarter. Finally, the Tigers had a third-down play with the ball at the Dartmouth three-yard line. That's when it happened.

A man wearing street clothes came splashing through the

Dartmouth end zone. He ran straight for the Dartmouth players, then took his place on the line between tackle Dave Camerer and guard Joe Handrahan. He was going to try to help with the goal line stand. Before the play got off, the mystery man leaped across the line and attempted to block a Princeton player. He fell flat on his face.

The Princeton players began roughing up the stranger, who was finally dragged off by two policemen. Princeton then scored the final touchdown to ensure a 26-6 victory. But after the game, no one could find Dartmouth's mystery "12th man."

Two men came forward to claim they were the intruder, but there was no proof that either was telling the truth. The mysterious 12th man was never found, even after Associated Press sports writers voted the incident the number-one oddity of 1935.

PASS 'EM SILLY

The forward pass was legalized in college football in 1906. That didn't mean, however, that a whole crop of John Elways, Joe Montanas, and Dan Marinos appeared overnight and began throwing the football all over the lot. On the contrary, passing was still limited and selective, and sometimes non-existent.

But things changed in a hurry on November 1, 1913, when the Fighting Irish of Notre Dame rolled into West Point to play powerful Army. It was the first big game for the Irish against a team from another part of the country. Army was an overwhelming favorite, but two Notre Dame players—quarterback Gus Dorais and receiver Knute Rockne—had other ideas.

Rockne, of course, would someday take over the coaching reins at Notre Dame and prove to be one of the most innovative football minds in the country. In the summer of 1913, he and Dorais got together and devised a sophisticated passing game, the likes of which had never been seen before. They decided to unveil it against Army.

It started early. In the first quarter, the clever Rockne pretended to have a leg injury from the previous play. At the next snap, he took off and Dorais hit him with a perfect, 25-yard touchdown pass. For the rest of the afternoon Dorais hit his targets in full stride, and a startled Army defense couldn't stop him. He wound up with 13 completions in 17 tries for 243 yards as Notre Dame won, 35-13.

Even more than that, the game showed just how effective a good passing game could be. It wouldn't happen overnight, but the forward pass would soon become a basic part of the college football scene.

SHORT TAKES ON THE COLLEGE GAME

The Lonely End. When the powerful Army team took the field in 1958, it showed a formation never seen before. Wide receiver Bill Carpenter never joined the huddle. He stood by himself, 15 yards away, getting the play through foot signals from his quarterback. He was dubbed "the lonely end" and was so good that he was named an All-American. Later, Carpenter became a war hero in Vietnam.

Cougar Blitz. Everything was going as expected at the Houston-Tulsa game on November 23, 1968. Early in the third quarter the favored Houston Cougars led, 24-6, and seemed headed for an easy win. What no one anticipated was the offensive explosion that followed. Houston scored four touchdowns in the third quarter and an incredible seven in the fourth. Counting 10 of 11 extra points, that made the final score an amazing 100-6.

One Too Many. In the closing moments of the 1969 Orange Bowl, unbeaten Penn State scored a touchdown to come within one point of Kansas at 14-13. Penn's Nittany Lions then tried to throw for the winning two-point conversion, only to have the ball batted away. But just a minute. A flag had been thrown. A sharp-eyed official made a quick count and realized that Kansas had 12 men on the field. Penn State was given another chance, allowing halfback Bob Campbell to punch the ball over for two points and a 15-14 Penn State win.

Some Kind of Hot. It didn't look like a good day for Texas-El Paso quarterback Brooks Dawson when he entered a 1967 game against

New Mexico. Dawson misfired on his first three passes. But, suddenly, he got the touch. Boy, did he ever. Dawson's next six passes all went for touchdowns! He wound up the day averaging 41.8 yards on nine completions and led his team to a 75-12 victory.

The Ghost Really Gallops. In a game against Michigan in 1924, Illinois halfback Red Grange took the opening kickoff back 95 yards for a score. Known as the Galloping Ghost for his broken-field runs, Grange had one of the most incredible first quarters ever. Following the kickoff return he scored on runs of 45, 55, and 67 yards. He was unstoppable. The most publicized college player of his time, Grange signed with the Bears but was never a superstar in the National Football League.

The Four Horsemen. Maybe the most legendary backfield in college football history was the Notre Dame quartet labeled "the Four Horsemen" by sportswriter Grantland Rice. They helped the Irish pile up a 27-2-1 record from 1922 to 24. Using speed, strength, and intelligence, they were an almost perfect unit. But compared to players today, they were small men. Halfbacks James Crowley and Donald Miller each weighed just 162 pounds. Fullback Elmer Layden was a 160-pounder, and quarterback Harry Stuhldreher tipped the scales at a mere 154.

The Tonawanda Terror. He came from Tonawanda, New York, stood just five-feet-five-inches tall, and weighed 145 pounds as a Yale freshman in 1891. Yet Frank Hinkey became one of greatest players of his time. He had astonishing speed and strength for a man of his size, often using his body to break down Harvard's murderous flying wedge. He never missed a game, and was an All-American for four straight years as Yale won 50 of 51 games. Yet the player nicknamed the Tonawanda Terror played four years with a horrible secret: he was suffering from a severe case of tuberculosis. Just a few years after starring at Yale, Frank Hinkey was dead.

Frosty's Foot. His real name was Forrest, but everyone always called him Frosty. In 1924 Frosty Peters was a quarterback and dropkicker for Montana State's freshman team. When the team took the field against Billings Polytechnic on a November afternoon, Frosty warmed up quickly. With his teammates setting him up, Frosty began drop-kicking field goals. By halftime, he had made nine of 14 three pointers. He kept kicking, and when the game ended he had a record 17 field goals in 22 attempts, good for 51 points in a 64-0 victory. It's still a record.

A Super Number. When the great Jim Brown came to Syracuse University he wore the number 44 on his uniform. After a magnificent career with the Orangemen, Brown left and another fine runner took his place. Ernie Davis also wore number 44 and was an All-American. Davis died tragically of leukemia before he was able to play pro ball. So when Floyd Little came to Syracuse a few years later, he asked for number 44 as a tribute to Brown and Davis. The legend continued: Little also became an All-American running back with the Orangemen. Seems as if number 44 just couldn't miss.

Heisman Winner In Six. One of the oddest choices for football's Heisman Trophy had to be Angelo Bertelli, the Notre Dame quarterback who won the award in 1943. Not because Bertelli wasn't an outstanding player. He was. Rather, it was that he only played six games that season. After leading the Irish to a 6-0 record and throwing 10 TD passes, Bertelli was ordered to report for training in the Marines. World War II was on and Bertelli went. The Heisman voters apparently still thought he was the best in the land that year, short season and all.

Magic Transformation. For two years Nolan Cromwell was a starting defensive back for the University of Kansas. But in the third game of his junior year, in 1975, he was moved to quarterback to run the Jawhawks' wishbone offense. All Cromwell did his first day at QB was rush for 294 yards on 28 carries, setting a rushing record for a quarterback and breaking the great Gale Sayers's Kansas rushing mark of 283 yards. Later, in the pros, Cromwell became an All-Pro safety.

Rose Bowl Jinx. For three straight years, from 1949 to 1951, the University of California was unbeaten in the regular season. Each time the Golden Bears received invitations to the Rose Bowl and each time they lost. Unbeaten seasons went down the drain at the hands of Northwestern, Ohio State, and Michigan.

Make up Your Mind. Speaking of the Rose Bowl, the game called the "granddaddy" of all bowl games started in 1902. But after one game football was unceremoniously dropped from the format at Tournament Park in Pasadena, California, not to return until 1916. One of the events that replaced the gridiron game was… get ready for this… chariot races!

Sharp-eyed Quarterback.
When the Washington Huskies made it to the Rose Bowl in both 1960 and 1961, they were led by quarterback Bob Schloredt. The Huskies topped Wisconsin in 1960, then beat top-ranked Minnesota the next year. Schloredt played so well that he shared Player of the Game honors in 1960 and won the prize outright in 1961. Yet Bob Schloredt played quarterback with a handicap. He hit his precision passes despite being virtually blind in one eye!

Winning After Losing. The Heisman Trophy is given annually to the college player considered the best in the land. On almost every occasion, the winner has come off an outstanding season with an outstanding team behind him. Not so in 1956. The winner that year was Paul Hornung, whom the voting committee decided had had a brilliant season at Notre Dame and deserved the award. Unfortunately, Hornung's Fighting Irish teammates didn't match his efforts. Notre Dame had a miserable 2-8 record that year, the only time a Heisman Trophy winner came from a losing team.

The Chinese Bandits. This was the name given to a special defensive unit at Louisiana State as the Tigers marched toward a national championship in 1958. Coach Paul Dietzel played three units that year. First, he had his regulars who started on both offense and defense. Then he had a "go" unit, which he brought in to give the club an offensive lift. And when he wanted to take the heart out of the opposition he went to his swarming, screaming, gung-ho defensive unit known as the Chinese Bandits. The nickname came from a Terry and the Pirates comic strip, and it caught on. The Chinese Bandits helped give Louisiana State's football team its identity, while at the same time spurring them to the top of the heap.

They Said It:
Memorable
Quotes From
the World of
Football

Here is a selection of memorable quotes from players and coaches down through the years. Some are amusing, others simply define the gridiron game the way the participants see it. All are fun to read and remember. Here football is football, the college and pro games combined.

"A man could get hurt
playing this game if he doesn't take care."

*The great Jim Thorpe to a fallen rival
after clobbering him with a furious tackle.*

"If you want a messenger,
make a call to Western Union."

*The unpredictable Joe Don Looney
of the Detroit Lions when his coach asked him to
bring a play in to the quarterback.*

"Gentleman, this is a football. Before we're
through we're gonna run it down
everybody's throats."

*Vince Lombardi at his first team meeting after
taking over as coach of the Green Bay Packers.*

"I was slugged in high school,
I was slugged in prep school, I was slugged at
Yale. But I was never slugged in the pros."

*Century Milstead commenting on the
relative roughness of football at each level.*

"Please drive carefully on your
way home. The life you save may be Abner Haynes."

*The public address announcer for
the old Dallas Texans of the AFL referring
to the team's star halfback and
most popular player, Abner Haynes.*

"**T**he Bears are crybabies.
When the going gets tough, the Bears quit."

*Washington Redskins owner
George Preston Marshall a day before
the Chicago Bears destroyed his team,
73-0, for the NFL crown in 1940.*

"**I**t was the best run I've had
in the NFL. To tell the truth, I didn't think of
what I was going to do.
I just let instinct take over."

*Marcus Allen of the Los Angeles Raiders after
making a 74-yard touchdown run in Super Bowl XVIII.*

"**W**e were going up against this
young kid and I thought it would be easy. Then
he started running around back there.
I had him one time, I thought... So I really cut
loose, and what happens? He's going
the other way and I'm tackling air. It was like
he had eyes in the back of his head...
unless he heard me huffing and puffing
behind him."

*Veteran Indianapolis Colts defensive end
Gino Marchetti on what it was like
chasing scrambling quarterback Fran Tarkenton
of the Vikings in 1961.*

"**I** saw him stripped down in the locker
room and I thought, God must
have taken a chisel and said, 'I'm gonna
make me a halfback.'"

*Chicago Bears backfield coach
Fred O'Connor on seeing future superstar
Walter Payton for the first time.*

"**H**e'll run as often as we
need him to run. And the more he runs,
the better he gets."

*University of Southern California coach
John McKay on the talent of his tail
back star O. J. Simpson, in 1967.*

"The attitude of the coach is very
important. He has to want to pass, then teach
it properly and be willing to work on
it by the hour. As far as I'm concerned, passing
is the best way to win football games,
because it's the only way you
can average nine or ten yards a play."

San Diego Chargers record-setting quarterback
Dan Fouts, describing his philosophy and how it
agreed with that of his coach, Don Coryell.

"The first catch was incredible,
the second unbelievable, the third was merely
a standard, difficult professional reception.
The fourth was a blazing touchdown that
earned Swann Most Valuable Player honors."

One of the sportswriters who witnessed
Pittsburgh star Lynn Swann's four catches for
161 yards against the Cowboys in Super Bowl X.

"Football players are human, too.
We function on emotions. As soon as you
stepped on that field… the fans
made you feel like you belonged."

Mean Joe Greene, Steelers All-Pro defensive
tackle, on his reaction to the Pittsburgh fans.

"The first time I saw him
play I started packing my bags."

*The reaction of Bears veteran middle linebacker
Bill George when he saw rookie middle linebacker Dick Butkus in the Bears' training camp.*

"To be honest, I thought I could
do it all in one year, I really did. I didn't realize
that in pro football you start from scratch.
You have to relearn everything from
the very beginning. It's a brand new ball
game all the way."

*Hall of Fame quarterback Terry Bradshaw
on the transition to pro ball after completing his
rookie year with the Steelers.*

"I do some of my best thinking
at the piano after a hard game, unless my
hands are so beat up I can't play
properly. Somehow, the exhaustive emotion of
a football game brings out a whole different
set of emotions for my composing."

*Cincinnati Bengals All-Pro defensive tackle Mike
Reid talking about combining football and music.
He would retire from football at the age of 27 to
concentrate on music full-time.*

"The league can't stand many more events of this kind and expect to be taken seriously by the public. The league revealed itself to be definitely small-time. For a day, at least, professional football slipped back into its unsavory past and did itself incalculable harm."

Sportswriter Stanley Woodward commenting on the 1939 NFL title game between the Packers and the Giants that was played at the old State Fair Park in Milwaukee. The stadium was bad, there were problems with fake tickets, and front-row patrons had to sit on uncomfortable folding chairs. Woodward obviously couldn't envision what the game would be like in another 50 years.

"This is the greatest team I've ever been associated with. It's hard to compare it with other great teams but this team has gone into an area no other team has ever gone into before. It went through the season undefeated and won it at the end."

Coach Don Shula on his 1972 Miami Dolphins team finishing the season unbeaten and then winning the Super Bowl. They were the first ever to do it.

"I thought it was too high.
I don't jump that well and I was real tired.
I had the flu last week and I had trouble
getting my breath on the last drive. I don't
know how I caught the ball."

*Dwight Clark of the San Francisco 49ers after he
made a last-second leaping catch of a Joe
Montana pass to give the 49ers a 28-27 victory
over Dallas in the 1981 NFC title game.
Niner fans still refer to it as "the Catch."*

"I lived one hundred years for the
next few seconds because all of a sudden it
dawned on me, 'You crazy nut! You have
the ball down there now and you want to take
a chance on someone fumbling it on this
frozen ground just to move it
in a little better position.'"

*Cleveland Browns quarterback Otto Graham on
running a quarterback sneak just prior to Lou
Groza's 16-yard field goal that won the 1950 NFL
title over the Los Angeles Rams.*

"We were so darned disgusted
with ourselves that when we got the ball for
that last series, we struck back
at the Giants in a sort of blind fury."

*Baltimore Colts quarterback John Unitas com-
menting on his team's mood after the Giants had
taken a 17-14 lead late in the fourth quarter of
the 1958 championship game. The Colts went on
to win, 23-17.*

"The Giants' coaches keyed Huff
on me quite a bit. He played hard but not dirty.
I think there was only one game where
he got out of line and twisted my head at the
bottom of a pile. 'That's not like you,
Huff,' I told him. Normally, I wouldn't even tell
an opponent he was overdoing it. But
in Sam's case, I figured he might appreciate my
opinion because we'd been slamming each
other since college."

*Cleveland running back Jim Brown on his person-
al rivalry with Giants' linebacker Sam Huff.*

"Jim Brown was a phenomenal
running back, the greatest who ever
played. I am proud to have played on the same
field with him. No matter how hard you hit
him, he never said a harsh word. But when you
hit him, it was like hitting an oak tree."

Sam Huff on his personal rivalry with Jim Brown.

"**Y**ou could feel the tension in
the dressing room the moment the players
arrived. There was dead silence.
No one said a word to anyone because they
had pitched themselves so high. Usually I
would say something before a game, but that
day I knew there was nothing to say.
All I did was open the door and say, 'Let's go.'
It was a day when the Lions
could have beaten any team they played."

Coach George Wilson of the Detroit Lions com-
menting on the emotional high his team experi-
enced before beating the powerful Green Bay
Packers, 26-14, in their traditional Thanksgiving
Day game in 1962.

"**W**e didn't play any bush
leaguers, and we were happy to accomplish
what we did. You could practically hear
the giant sigh of relief in the dressing room
when the game was over."

Green Bay safety Willie Wood talking for his
Packer teammates after they had beaten the
Kansas City Chiefs in Super Bowl I.

"**W**e didn't lose. We just ran
out of time."

Cincinnati Bengals coach Forrest Gregg after his
team was beaten by the San Francisco 49ers,
26-21, in Super Bowl XVI.

"**W**e felt he'd be a superstar all along. He had the six qualities we used to determine a superstar running back— speed, shiftiness, balance, strength, size, and the most important, the instinct to make the right move at the right time, do it automatically, even without thinking."

Chicago Bears owner and coach George Halas on his sensational rookie running back out of Kansas, Gale Sayers, in 1965.

Gridbits
Little-Known Gridiron Facts

In the long history of football there are bound to be those little extras, bits and pieces of information that aren't in the mainstream of the sport. These "gridbits" make fun reading, and also can give you ideas for trivia questions with which to stump your friends. See how many of them you've heard before.

Former President Ronald Reagan was always a big football fan, and with good reason. Not only did Mr. Reagan play the game at Eureka College in Illinois, he later became a sportscaster in Des Moines, Iowa. But perhaps the football memory most associated with him was his role as George Gipp, the legendary Notre Dame halfback, in the film *Knute Rockne, All American*.

Another famous football film biography was *Jim Thorpe, All-American*. Playing the role of the great Indian athlete was one of the most athletic of actors, Burt Lancaster.

Many former football players have made their marks in other fields. Byron "Whizzer" White was an All-American halfback at the University of Colorado in 1937. He later became an All-Pro running back for the Detroit Lions. After that, how-

Ronald Reagan as the Gipper

ever, White went to law school and at the age of 44 was appointed an associate justice of the United States Supreme Court.

Take a look at the college football record book. A UCLA halfback is listed as the fourth best career punt returner in NCAA history, with an average of 18.8 yards a return. He played back in 1939-1940 before turning to another sport—baseball. Seven years later Jackie Robinson made history by becoming the first black man to play in the major leagues.

In 1954, a Florida State freshman known as Buddy Reynolds carried the ball 16 times for 134 yards, and also caught four passes for another 76 yards. He then went on to letter with the varsity in 1955 and 1957. Soon after that he gave up football for acting, and became known to the world as Burt Reynolds.

When coach Jimmy Johnson led the Dallas Cowboys to Super Bowl crowns in January 1993 and in January 1994, he became the only man in football to achieve an unusual triple triumph. He was a player on the Arkansas national championship team in 1964, then coached the Miami Hurricanes to a national collegiate championship in 1987, and completed the triple when he guided the Cowboys to their Super Bowl triumphs.

U.S. president Theodore Roosevelt, an avid horseman, soldier, hunter, and outdoorsman, threatened to outlaw football in 1906 because the sport had become too violent. His concern led to rule changes to modify the mayhem.

One of the top players on the 1945 Indiana team that had a 9-0-1 record was end Ted Kluszewski. Big Klu caught three TD passes during the year, but later made his mark in another sport. He became the slugging first baseman of the Cincinnati Reds and hit 279 home runs before retiring.

Two other U.S. presidents who played college football were Richard Nixon and Gerald Ford. Mr. Nixon was a reserve for Whittier College in California; Mr. Ford was an outstanding center on the 1934 Michigan team and played in the college all-star game against the Chicago Bears in 1935.

There was also a U.S president who once played against Jim Thorpe. Dwight D. Eisenhower was a starting halfback on the 1912 Army team that went up against Thorpe and Carlisle College. Carlisle won, 27-6, and a

Gerald Ford

week later Eisenhower suffered a career-ending knee injury in a game against Tufts.

What's it like to replace a legend? When Notre Dame's Knute Rockne was killed in a plane crash in 1931, the new coach was Heartley Anderson. He lasted just three years and had a record of 16-9-2. Phil Bengston fared even worse. He was the man who replaced Vince Lombardi at Green Bay just as the dynasty was crumbling. Bengston coached for three years to the tune of a 20-21-1 mark.

A couple of ex-footballers made more of a reputation riding horses than galloping on the gridiron. Johnny Mack Brown, who played for Alabama in the 1926 Rose Bowl, later found his way to Hollywood where he starred in a number of low-budget westerns.

At the same time a tall, strapping youngster named Marion Morrison was playing for Southern Cal. After the 1926 season Morrison headed out to Hollywood. Unlike Brown, Morrison decided to change his name. In the movies he became internationally known as John Wayne.

On January 10, 1982, the San Diego Chargers met the Cincinnati Bengals at Riverfront Stadium in Cincy for the AFC championship. The Bengals won, 27-7, under conditions that weren't exactly perfect. It was so cold in Cincinnati that day that the game was almost called off. It was played, however, forcing players, officials, and spectators to endure a wind-chill factor of 59 degrees below zero!

There was something very different about the Rose Bowl game between Oregon

John Wayne at Southern Cal.

State and Duke on January 1, 1942. Because Pearl Harbor in Hawaii had been bombed by the Japanese just three weeks before, it was deemed unsafe to have large crowds gather on the West Coast. The game was played instead at the Duke campus in Durham, North Carolina, the only Rose Bowl ever that was not played in Pasadena.

Want proof that Yale University was a football power in the early days of the game? The Elis have produced the most consensus All-Americans of any school. The count is at an even 100. Yet the 100th and last player to be added to this impressive list was end Paul Walker. And that was way back in 1944.

Kansas was visiting Texas Tech in Lubbock on September 18, 1965. By the time the fourth quarter rolled around Texas Tech was comfortably ahead, 26-7, when officials were suddenly told to stop the game right away. Seems there was a tornado alert in the Lubbock area and authorities wanted the stadium cleared. Texas Tech was declared the winner and everybody was sent home.

When the University of Houston racked up its incredible 100-6 victory over Tulsa in 1968, a reserve wide receiver caught a 26-yard touchdown pass in the final quarter. His name was Larry Gatlin, and he went on to find fame as a member of the country and western group The Gatlin Brothers.

George Halas's first entry in the 1920 league that would become the NFL was called the Decatur Staleys. Two years later the team became the Chicago Bears. But that first year Decatur had a feisty little quarterback who fought and scrapped for everything. Charley Dressen wasn't a great football

**Country and western singer
Larry Gatlin**

Quarterback Doug Flutie

player. So he moved on to base-ball, first as a player, then as a manager who guided the Brooklyn Dodgers to a pair of pennants in the 1950s. One of the greatest baseball pitchers of all time also played the gridiron game. Before he won 373 games for the New York Giants, Christy Mathewson was a turn-of-the-century star for Bucknell University, where he excelled as a dropkicker.

The name isn't always the same. Back in the 1960s, Eastern Kentucky had a two-way end named Harvey Lee Yeary. A back injury shortened his career and he graduated in 1963. After he resurfaced in Hollywood as a television actor named Lee Majors he rose to fame in series such as *The Six Million Dollar Man*.

Two great quarterbacks engineered college football's greatest aeri-al shootout on November 23, 1984. Boston College's Doug Flutie com-pleted 34 of 46 passes for 472 yards, while Miami's Bernie Kosar hit on 25 of 38 for 447 yards. It was so close that it took a last-second, 64-yard miracle "Hail Mary" pass by Flutie to Gerard Phelan to win it, 47-45.

The wrong man was given credit for a dramatic last-second victory on January 2, 1956. Soon after Michigan State beat UCLA, 17-14, in the Rose Bowl on a 41-yard field goal in the final seven seconds, word went out nationwide that Gerry Planutis had booted the game-winner. About 15 minutes later, however, it was learned that long-range kicker Dave Kaiser was the one who had powered the ball through the goal-posts. So much for instant fame.

Cal Hubbard, who played in the NFL for the New York Giants, Green Bay Packers, and old Pittsburgh Pirates, was inducted into the Pro Football Hall of Fame in 1963. That wasn't all. The same year he was inducted into the National Football Foundation Hall of Fame for college players. After football ended, he became a major league baseball umpire, then the supervisor of umpires, and was elected to the Baseball Hall of Fame in 1976, the only man to receive pro football's, college football's, and baseball's highest honors.

National Football League attendance is nothing like it used to be. In 1934, the first year records were kept, a total of 492,684 people attended NFL games, an average of 8,211 per game. In 1990 the league set a new record when 13,959,896 people rolled through the turnstiles. That's an average of 62,321 per game. It's a growing game, all right.

Many of the most watched programs in television history have been Super Bowl telecasts. In fact, Super Bowl XXVIII (Bills vs. Cowboys) was viewed by 42,860,000 U.S. households.

The Language of the Game

Every sport has its own special terminology. To fully understand a sport it's necessary to know what the players, officials, commentators, and writers mean when they use expressions that are unique to the game. Here is a basic glossary of football terms that will help you to better understand and follow the game.

Blitz—A play in which several defensive players (usually linebackers and defensive backs) rush the quarterback instead of covering their normal defensive positions. Also called a red dog.

Bomb—A slang term used to describe a very long pass thrown far downfield by the quarterback. It is usually intended to gain big chunks of yardage or to score a touchdown on a single play.

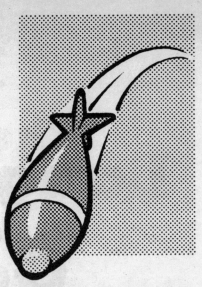

Chains—These are used to mark and measure for a first down. They are exactly ten yards long and have a stick and flag on each end so they can be seen by the players and spectators. If the referee cannot tell by looking whether a first down has been made, he will call for a closer measurement and the chains will be brought onto the field.

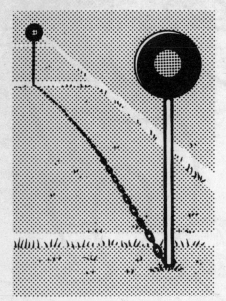

Clipping—A common violation in which a player throws his body across the back of an opponent's leg or hits him from the back below the waist while moving up from behind. Exceptions are if the opponent is running with the ball or the action is in close-line play.

Crackback—A dangerous and illegal block in which an eligible receiver set two yards or more outside the tackle comes back and throws a block below the waist from the blind side.

Crossbar—The horizontal bar between the goalposts. The ball must pass over the crossbar and between the vertical uprights for an extra point or field goal to be good.

Cut or Cutback—A quick change of direction by a ballcarrier in an attempt to avoid a tackler.

Dead ball—Any ball not in play. The ball becomes dead once the official blows his whistle to end a play.

Delay of game—A violation called when the offensive team fails to get a play off within 40 seconds of the referee's signal to put the ball in play.

Direct snap—The exchange of the football between the center and the quarterback when the QB stands several yards behind the center in a shotgun-type formation. The center can also direct snap to the punter or the holder for a placekick. If the quarterback is standing directly over the center, it's simply called the snap.

Down—The term used to number the plays in each sequence during the game. An offensive team has four downs in which to make ten yards. If they make the ten yards or more on any down, they begin over again with another first down.

Drop back—The quick retreat the quarterback makes when he is getting ready to pass. The quarterback usually drops back about seven yards after taking the snap from the center. This gives his receivers time to get downfield.

Encroachment—A violation when a player enters the neutral zone and makes contact with an opponent before the ball is snapped.

End zone—The ten-yard area beyond each goal line in which a touchdown can be scored. Teams can advance the ball into the end zone by running or passing.

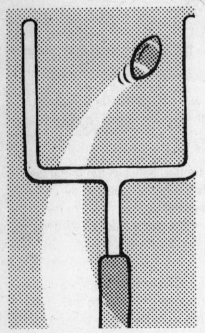

Extra point—After each touchdown, a team has the option of either attempting an extra point kick or running or passing the ball into the end zone for two points. The ball is placed at the two-yard line, and most teams will try to placekick it over the crossbar of the goalposts.

Fair catch—An unhindered catch of a kick by a member of the receiving team, who must raise one arm a full length above his head while the kick is in the air. The kicking team cannot interfere with the catch, but if the ball is dropped either team can recover it.

Field goal—A scoring play is made when the offensive team placekicks the ball through the goalposts and over the crossbar. It counts three points and can be tried from any place on the field and on any down.

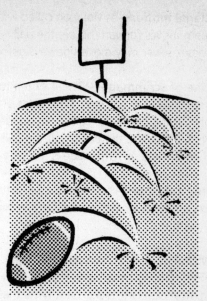

Fumble—The dropping of the football by an offensive player during a play. The free ball can then be recovered by either team. A defensive player can cause a fumble by slapping or grabbing at the ball, but if a player loses the ball when he hits the ground, it is not a fumble but a dead ball.

Handoff—The exchange of the football between the quarterback and a running back. The quarterback hands the ball off as the back runs past him. It takes practice and timing to do it right.

Huddle—A circle made by the offensive team back from the line of scrimmage in which they plan the next play.

I-formation—A formation used more in colleges than in the pros in which the two running backs are lined up one behind the other and directly behind the quarterback.

Illegal motion—A violation called when a member of the offensive team moves forward before the ball is snapped. A running back or pass receiver may move sideways before the snap, but not forward.

Line of scrimmage—Wherever the football is placed on the field, an imaginary line runs from both sides of the ball to the sidelines. It divides the offensive team from the defensive unit and indicates the yard line where the ball sits. If the ball is three yards beyond the 20, then the line of scrimmage is the 23-yard line.

Neutral zone—The space between the two ends of the football as it sits on the field. Both the offensive and defensive teams must remain behind their end of the ball.

Nickel back—An extra defensive back put into the game in certain passing situations, usually when there is an extra pass receiver in the lineup. In most cases the nickel back takes the place of a linebacker. A second extra defensive back is sometimes called a dime back.

Offside— A violation that occurs when any part of a player's body is beyond the line of scrimmage when the ball is snapped.

Option Play—A name given to a play in which the quarterback has a choice whether to run or pass.

Passing combination—A quarterback and pass receiver who work very well together. John Unitas to Raymond Berry was a great passing combination of the 1950s and 1960s. Troy Aikman to Michael Irvin is a great combination today.

Penalty—A loss of yardage by either team as the result of a violation of the rules.

Pitchout—A play where the quarterback flips the ball underhanded to a running back who is too far from him to take a handoff. It is also called a lateral.

Placekick—A kickoff, extra point, or field goal in which the ball is kicked while being held in a fixed position on the ground or sitting on a kicking tee.

Plane—An imaginary vertical line that goes straight up from the front of the goal line. An offensive player must break the plane of the goal line to score a touchdown. It is still a touchdown if he breaks the plane and is then pushed back before he hits the ground.

Pocket—An area in which the quarterback is protected by a circle of blockers as he gets ready to pass. Also called the passing pocket.

Pro set—The standard NFL formation with two running backs split several feet apart behind the quarterback.

Punt—A kick used to move the football downfield, usually when the offensive team has a fourth down deep in its own territory. The punter stands about 15 yards behind the line of scrimmage, takes a long snap from center, then releases the ball and boots it before it hits the ground.

Read—To read a play is to know what kind of play is coming before it happens. Both offensive and defensive players can "read" each other by watching formations and player movements very carefully.

Return—A term used to describe carrying the football after it has been exchanged from one team to the other by a kickoff, punt, interception, or fumble recovery. It is also called a runback.

Safety—A scoring play that counts two points and occurs when a member of the offensive team is tackled with the football in the end zone behind his own goal line.

Shift—The legal movement of two or more offensive players at the same time before the snap. A shift is used to confuse the defense just before the snap.

Shotgun—An offensive formation in which the quarterback stands five or six yards behind the center and takes a direct snap from that point. It is usually used in passing situations so that the quarterback is ready to throw sooner.

Special teams—Players who see action on the kickoff, kickoff return, placekick, punt, and punt return units. A player can be on the regular offensive or defensive units and still play on special teams. Others might play only on special teams.

Sudden death—Term used to describe the extra period played when the game is tied after regulation play. It is called sudden death (or sudden victory) because the game ends as soon as one team scores by means of a touchdown, field goal, or safety.

Suicide squad—A nickname given to the special teams because of the high-speed collisions and very hard hitting during kicks and kick returns.

Sweep—Name given to an offensive running play in which the running back carries the ball wide toward the sideline while following one or two blocking linemen. As soon as his linemen open up a "hole" in the defense, the runner turns, or "cuts," upfield to gain as many yards as he can.

Three-point stance—The starting position for most interior linemen before a play. Each player squats down low, feet spread apart, with his weight balanced on an arm that touches the ground. The two feet and one hand on the ground make up the three points of the stance.

Touchback—A nonscoring play that occurs when the ball is called dead on or behind a team's own goal line, provided it is not a touchdown. A defensive player fielding a punt, intercepting a pass, or picking up a fumble in the end zone has the option of running the ball out or simply kneeling down on one knee for a touchback. The ball is then placed on the 20-yard line, where the team getting the touchback puts it into play.

Touchdown—A scoring play is made when any part of the ball in possession of a player is on, above, or over the opponents' goal line. It's worth six points and can be made by running or throwing the ball into the end zone, or by recovering a fumble in the opponents' end zone.

Two-point conversion—After each touchdown, a team can attempt to run or pass the ball into the end zone from the two-yard line for two points (instead of attempting an extra-point kick).

Wishbone—A formation used mainly in college football in which the fullback is directly behind the quarterback and two additional running backs are behind him, each split to one side, giving the formation a "Y" or wishbone look.

Zebras—The nickname given to the on-field officials because of the traditional black-and-white striped shirts they always wear.

The Officials

Speaking of zebras, there are seven officials at each NFL game. Let's take a quick look at them and some of the things they do during the course of a game.

1. Referee. The referee has general overall control of the game. He gives the signals for all fouls and violations and is the final authority for all rule interpretations and questions. He usually positions himself in the backfield 10 to 12 yards behind the line of scrimmage and favors the right side if the quarterback is right-handed.

The referee determines the legality of the snap and observes the deep backs for illegal motion. He also watches the quarterback on running plays during and after the hand-off, remains with him until the action has cleared, then proceeds downfield, checking on the runner and the contact behind him. On pass plays the referee drops back with the quarterback and determines the legality of the blocks by nearby linemen. He is primarily responsible for "roughing the passer" calls (when the passer is tackled after he has thrown or handed off the ball) and for making judgments on loose balls. The referee also spots the ball (places it on the line of scrimmage) after each play.

2. Umpire. The umpire rules on players' conduct and actions on the scrimmage line. He stands four or five yards downfield and looks for possible false starts by offensive linemen. He also observes the legality of contact by both the offensive and defensive linemen; he moves forward on pass plays to ensure that interior linemen do not move illegally downfield; and he assists in ruling on incomplete or trapped passes when the ball is thrown long or short. In addition, it is the umpire's responsibility to see that players use only regulation equipment on the field.

3. Head linesman. His primary responsibility is to rule on offsides, encroachment (illegal advances), and other actions at the line of scrimmage prior to and at the snap. He also watches defenders to see if

they illegally interfere with receivers, and has the full responsibility to rule on sideline plays on his side of the field. He is also responsible for keeping track of downs and the mechanics of the chain crew.

4. Line judge. The line judge straddles the line of scrimmage on the side of the field opposite the head linesman. He keeps the time of the game as a backup for the clock operator. He also helps with offsides and encroachment calls, as well as actions at the line of scrimmage at the snap. The line judge rules on whether or not the passer is behind or beyond the line of scrimmage when he releases the ball.

5. Back judge. He is on the same side of the field as the line judge, but 20 yards deep. He watches the wide receiver on his side and also concentrates on the path of the end or back, making sure that the blocks are legal. He also makes decisions involving catching, recovery, or illegal touching of a loose ball beyond the line of scrimmage.

6. Side judge. The side judge operates on the same side of the field as the head linesman, but 20 yards deep. His responsibilities are similar to those of the back judge.

7. Field judge. The field judge takes a position 25 yards downfield. In general, he favors the tight end's side of the field. He concentrates on the tight end's path, watching for legal or illegal blocks thrown by and against him. He also times the intervals between plays and the intermissions between each quarter. In addition, he calls pass interference, fair-catch infractions, and clipping violations on kick returns. He and the back judge rule whether or not field goals and conversions are successful.

Officials must work together as a team to keep a game running smoothly. If there is a questionable play or call, they must huddle together and quickly make a decision. They must also keep games from getting overly rough, stop occasional fights, and decide which, if any, players should be thrown out of the game.

19

The **Art**

of the

Game

Make no mistake about it, the game of football requires considerable skills. Some people prefer to call quarterback, running back, and receiver the "skill" positions. But linemen today are more than just brutes. They must know various blocking techniques and how to execute them. Defensive linemen, linebackers, and defensive backs must be able to "read" the offense and react to whatever comes at them. Plus, all football players must be tough.

In this chapter we will look at some of the basic skills that must be learned to play this complex sport.

QUARTERBACK

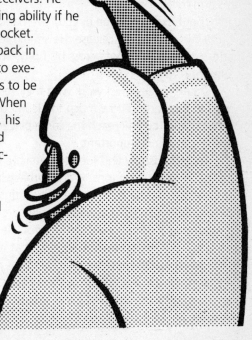

A quarterback today must be strong and also quick on his feet. He has to be able to take the snap from center and hand off smoothly to his backs. If he drops back to pass he must do it quickly and look downfield to spot his receivers. He should also have some running ability if he has to scramble out of the pocket.

But above all, a quarterback in today's game must be able to execute a passing attack. He has to be able to throw the football. When a quarterback holds the ball, his pinky and ring fingers should grip the laces tightly. The second finger should be placed just above the laces and the index finger up near the end of the ball. Fingers should be spread apart as far as possible.

The correct throwing motion is also important.

When the quarterback spots his target he brings his arm back from ear level to behind his head. A right-handed thrower will step into the pass with his left foot. He should turn his hips in the direction of the throw, his arm following.

The throw should be directly overhand with the arm snapping it off at the moment of release. He should follow through by bringing his arm straight down, not across his body. This motion will help ensure a straight throw.

Quarterbacks must work with their receivers. They must know how hard to throw, and how much to "lead" them so that the moving receiver and the ball reach the same place at the same time. Instinct and accuracy are important.

Terry Bradshaw and Joe Montana are two quarterbacks who had perfect throwing motions. A quarterback like Dan Marino has such a strong arm that he can get the ball off quickly with little more than a flick of the wrist. He has what is called a quick release. Bernie Kosar is a quarterback who breaks all the rules. He throws sidearm and across his body. But he has done it so long that he can make it work.

Quarterbacks must throw all kinds of passes—short and long, hard and soft, on a line and high in the air. This means practice, practice, and more practice. It takes a top NFL quarterback many years to become an All-Pro.

RUNNING BACK

Running backs need speed, quickness, and power. They also need a
special instinct for the running game. Like top running backs Gale
Sayers, O. J. Simpson, Barry Sanders, and Emmitt Smith, their split-sec-
ond "moves" and cuts must come naturally.

Vince Lombardi, the great Packer coach, said that a good back
always "runs to daylight." That means he sees the hole in the line and
can burst through it. In fact, a sudden burst of speed can always get a
running back extra yards.

Running backs must learn to take handoffs from the quarterback
smoothly and without hesitation. Timing is important. The back must
scoot past the quarterback just as the QB is turning to give him the
ball. The runner makes a pocket with his arms, raising the arm closest
to the quarterback across his chest. He keeps his other arm level across
his stomach. When the quarterback places the ball right in his stomach
area, the running back hugs it to his body, one hand on the top, the
other hand on the bottom.

If he is running directly into the line, he must hold the ball tightly
with both hands. Defenders will grab and slap at it. In the open field
he can carry with one arm, but should hold the ball close to his body
with his hand and forearm. Runners must also practice fakes and cuts.
To make a sharp cut they must plant one leg on the turf, push off, and
go the other way.

A good runner must also learn to follow his blockers. If the blocker
is pushing the defender to the right, the runner must cut left. He must
also learn to block for his quarterback and for another runner behind
him. It takes practice to master all these skills. Running fast or running
hard is not enough.

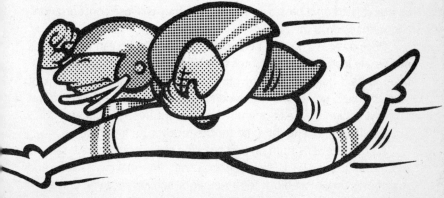

PASS RECEIVER

Speed, moves and fakes, good hands, fearlessness, and the ability to run are all necessary for a good pass receiver. Receivers must find a way to get "open," to get free of the defensive player or players guarding them. Wide receivers are usually very fast and can catch the ball over the middle or deep. The tight end is a bigger man who sometimes blocks like a lineman but must also catch the ball like the other receivers.

Pass receivers need what is called "soft hands." The hands must be relaxed with fingers spread wide. Receivers must let the ball settle into their hands, giving with it as it arrives. If they fight the ball with tense and tight hands, chances are it will bounce away. Relaxed hands make it easier to catch any type of pass——high, low, hard, soft, or over the shoulder.

Receivers also have to "look" the ball into their hands. They must focus or concentrate on catching the ball and nothing else. If they worry about the defensive back running alongside them or about being hit hard on a pass over the middle, they will lose concentration and perhaps drop the ball.

Once a receiver knows he can catch fearlessly, he can work on his moves. He learns the pass routes that his team runs and practices them. If he is going to run downfield and cut to the sideline, he might fake as if he is going over the middle, then cut to the sideline. A good fake made with the head or entire body might freeze a defender for just a split second, enough time for the receiver to get open.

A pass receiver's running and blocking skills should be the same as those of a running back. Receivers must run after making a catch, and sometimes they must block for a runner or another receiver. Once a receiver and quarterback work well together they become known as a passing combination. A good passing combination is hard to beat.

LINEMAN

In some ways being a lineman is the toughest job in football. Linemen collide with other linemen on every play. Offensive linemen must block for their quarterback and running backs. Defensive linemen must fight off blocks to make tackles and rush the passer. Playing the line is often called playing in the "trenches" (a term associated with warfare). Linemen don't always get the recognition that the quarterbacks, runners, receivers, linebackers, and defensive backs get.

Linemen must be big, quick, and strong. In fact, they must work to be the quickest and strongest they can be. Offensive linemen must learn the different blocking techniques. They have to be able to take a defensive lineman one way or the other on the running play, or just hold him at bay on passing plays. This requires good balance and a low center of gravity.

Defensive linemen can use their hands while offensive linemen cannot. Defensive linemen must have strong leg drive and use a variety of moves to get past their opponent in the trenches. Sometimes a lineman will just try to overpower his opponent. Sometimes he has to use moves, spinning and faking. Other times he can use speed to burst around or past an opponent.

Playing the line means all-out war on every play. It's a rough job and by the end of the game these 275-300 pound men are very tired.

LINEBACKER

Linebacker is not an easy position to play in today's game. A linebacker must be big and strong enough to jump onto the line of scrimmage and rush the passer. He also has to be quick enough to cover pass receivers and run down backs on sweeps. And he must have enough toughness to fight off blocks and make tackles in the middle. So he needs a combination of all the defensive skills.

On most plays, a linebacker sets up a few feet behind the line of scrimmage. But sometimes he also gets right up on the line in a three-point stance. Some teams use a middle linebacker and two outside linebackers. This is a 4-3 defense, because there are four down linemen. Others use two inside and two outside linebackers and only three down linemen. This is called a 3-4 defense.

As a rule, the middle or inside linebackers are bigger and better at stopping the run. The outside linebackers are quicker and can chase down runners or pass receivers. So a linebacker must always be in top physical condition. He is going to do a lot of running and hitting during a game.

He can work with the linemen on learning to fight off blocks and with the defensive backs on covering pass receivers. A linebacker must always be a good tackler, as well. There's no doubt that a smart and skilled linebacker can be a great help to any team's defense.

DEFENSIVE BACK

Speed and quickness are the two things a defensive back needs most. But he also needs the toughness to take on blockers and make tackles in the open field. Most teams have four defensive backs, two cornerbacks who play behind and to the outside of the outside linebackers, and two safeties who play deeper than the cornerbacks and toward the middle of the field.

The strong safety is usually the biggest and strongest of the defensive backs. He usually covers the tight end. The free safety must be very fast because he helps out wherever he's needed and has to use speed and instinct to be at the right spot at the right time.

Defensive backs often must move backward to cover a receiver. They must be able to move backward or laterally across the field and change direction in an instant. The advantage is with the receiver coming straight toward them, so they have to be able to take crossover steps and make a variety of quick moves.

The defensive back must stay close enough to the receiver to either knock the pass away or intercept it. If he makes contact with the receiver too soon he is called for pass interference, a violation. When this happens the pass is ruled complete and the offensive team given a first down. A pass interference penalty can be devastating to a defensive unit. The defensive back is also not permitted to block the vision of a receiver. That is called "face guarding" and also results in a penalty.

Defensive backs must focus on the situation at hand. If a defensive back is "burned" for a touchdown by a receiver, the whole stadium knows it. The defensive back must put this behind him quickly and continue to play his game. If he worries about it, it will probably happen again.

Every position on the football field is important. All require special skills and hours of practice to learn and master. Football is not a game to be taken lightly. There are many injuries each year, and players have to be alert and in peak physical condition. This will help them avoid injury.

But football is also a very rewarding and popular game. Just ask the millions of people who watch high school, college, and professional football each weekend during the season. They love it, and so do those who play.

CHAPTER
20

Football
A to Z

This is a kind of fun way of bringing things to a close—a quick
look at some more football, only this time with an
A to Z theme. It's also a good way to review some of the
things we've already talked about, add some new elements, and once
again look at the history of the game in an informative and entertaining
fashion. After all, the gridiron game is special, all the way from A to Z.

A America's Team, the nickname given to the Dallas Cowboys. It took on added significance in the early 1990s. Having won the Super Bowl in January 1993, and again in January 1994, the young Cowboys are the early favorites to become the "team of the 1990s," following the Packers in the 1960s, the Steelers in the 1970s and the 49ers in the 1980s.

B Bowl games. They get bigger and better every year. They now include the originals——the Rose, Orange, Cotton, and Sugar Bowls. Add to that the Gator, Florida Citrus, Liberty, John Hancock, Peach, Fiesta, Independence, Holiday, California, Aloha, Freedom, Hall of Fame, Copper, and Blockbuster Bowls, and there is a wealth of post season college football fun for everyone.

C What else but the Chicago Bears? What a great old franchise; what a tradition. Halas, Grange, Luckman, Nagurski, Sayers, Butkus, Atkins, McMahon, Dent, Singletary, Ditka, Payton. That's but a few of many. They were the Monsters of the Midway back in the early days and they're still the Monsters of the Midway today.

D Dan, as in Dan Marino. The Miami Dolphin quarterback is on a pace to break most of the passing records that are now in the book. In fact, he's cracked some already, such as his 48 touchdown passes in 1984. If he stays healthy, most of the major career marks will be his.

E Eric Dickerson, one of the greatest backs ever, who never seems to get enough credit for his achievements. He finished his career second to Walter Payton with more than 13,000 rushing yards to his credit. Any back with the talent and durability to rack up that kind of yardage has to be Hall of Fame material.

F Football as an international sport. The NFL is trying to spread its product worldwide. While football has always been wholly American, with a slight variation of the game played in Canada, it is slowly gaining popularity in other countries. In recent years exhibition games have been played by NFL teams in Britain, Japan, Sweden, Mexico, and Germany.

G George Gipp. Of all the stories from football's hallowed past, this is the one that seems to grip the imagination the most. "Win one for the Gipper" is an expression even non-football fans seem to know. It all happened so long ago and Gipp died so young. Of course, it didn't hurt that Ronald Reagan, who portrayed Gipp in the movies, was elected president in 1980. "The Gipper," George Gipp's nickname, became a popular nickname for Reagan, too.

H The Heisman Trophy. It remains college football's most prestigious award. Speculation about possible winners begins early in the season and doesn't stop. Even the presentation ceremony has become a media event with several of the top candidates invited to attend. Mention the "Heisman" and everyone knows just what you mean.

I Injuries have always been a part of football. But the advances in modern sports medicine have been amazing. Any kind of knee surgery used to finish a player for the year, maybe forever. Now knees are "scoped" regularly, the players walk out of the hospital, and are back on the field in weeks. All teams have the finest in training and medical facilities right in their stadiums.

J Jim Brown, the only player in the game who is still almost unanimously called the greatest at his position. He played from 1957 to 1965, and most of his records have been topped by other running backs, yet Brown is still remembered as the best running back who ever played. That in itself is an amazing testimonial to a great athlete.

K Kickers, kickers everywhere. They don't always feel like a real part of the team. But how many games have been won by a last-second field goal? Instant hero. And how many have been lost when that field goal was just wide? Total goat. Kickers often hold the key to the game in their accurate feet. They deserve credit for remaining cool in the pressure-cooker in which they must perform.

L Longest game played in the NFL. On December 25, 1971, the Miami Dolphins and Kansas City Chiefs played one full 15-minute overtime and 7:40 of a second OT period before Miami's Garo Yepremian settled the issue with a 32-yard field goal. But we just told you about kickers. At 82:40, it was the longest and one of the best.

M Mr. Montana. Not enough homage has been paid to quarterback Joe, called by many the best ever. Joe Montana has the highest quarterback rating of all time, has led his team to four Super Bowl triumphs, and has made the last-second comeback into a gridiron art.

N National champion, the most prestigious title in college football. It's still voted on by several different groups while the powers that be try to decide on a tournament format that would decide the national championship in a title game. That would simplify things, but even now being named national champion is a top goal for players and schools alike.

O Oorang Indians. Perhaps the oddest football team ever formed. The intent was good and its leader, Jim Thorpe, will always be a legend. But to put together a team allegedly made up of American Indians, then name it after a dog kennel, is something that wouldn't be tolerated today.

P Walter Payton. The NFL's all-time leading rusher possessed some amazing qualities. He was always in top condition, always ready to play, and always willing to take the ball as much as necessary. The team always came first before any individual records. Minor injuries, bumps, and bruises were ignored. There was no prima donna in him. No wonder he gained more than 16,000 yards in his career.

Q Quest for perfection. The thing that every coach and every team strives for at the beginning of a season. A perfect record. Undefeated. It's been done many times at the college level, but only once in the NFL by the 1972 Miami Dolphins. Yet the quest continues, renewed at the beginning of every new season.

R Rice as in Jerry Rice. Don't miss a chance to see this man in action. You may be watching the greatest wide receiver who ever played the game. And we're not the only ones saying it. He is a truly amazing athlete who seems to give a top-flight, All-Pro performance week in and week out.

S The Super Bowl, the single biggest spectacle in all of sports. The Super Bowl has become an American institution, almost always the most-watched television program of the year. How much of its attraction is in its name? It does have a ring to it. It's surely the pinnacle of football.

T Thurman Thomas, another of the superstars of the 1990s. The Buffalo Bills running back is a pleasure to watch. It's as if he was made for the description "the complete halfback." He can run, catch, and block. And he does it every week.

U Unitas, a name still revered in Baltimore and still remembered by football fans everywhere. Johnny U was a master quarterback who was a forerunner of the signal-callers of today. He had total confidence in his passing game and was deadly if his team trailed by just a few points late in the game.

V Vince Lombardi has been gone since 1970, yet is still considered the ideal pro football coach. He was a taskmaster and motivator. His players respected him totally, sometimes feared him, but always played their hearts out for him. Football was his life and he left the scene much too soon.

W World Football League. An attempt to start a rival pro league, the WFL played one full season in 1974, then died the following year. They tried to raid NFL talent and signed a couple of fine college players. But there was never any real chance that it could work.

X X's and O's. The traditional way a football coach diagrams plays on a blackboard. The X's stand for the players on one team, and the O's for the other team's players. A successful team, it is said, has its "X's and O's" down pat.

Y Yelberton Abraham Tittle, maybe the most unusual name for a Hall of Fame quarterback. No wonder everyone called him Y. A. But no one questioned his name when he threw seven touchdown passes in a single game or led the Giants to three straight NFL title games.

Z The Zendejas brothers. Four of the brothers have kicked in the National Football League. In 1991, Tony Zendejas became the first kicker in NFL history to go through an entire season without missing a field goal. Booting for the Los Angeles Rams, Zendejas made good on all 17 of his field-goal attempts, including a pair beyond the 50. A final bit of trivia before the gun sounds, ending the game.

INDEX

A

Adderley, Herb, 32, 67

Aikman, Troy, 79, 82, 152, 153
career summary, 127

Akron Pros, 147

Alabama, University of, 100,
150, 174, 181, 182, 183,
189, 192, 219
all-time record, 187
national champions, 174, 175

Aldrich, Ki, 150

Ali, Muhammad, 96

All-America Football Conference
(AAFC), 23, 34, 109, 143

Allegheny Athletic Association,
9-10

Allen, George, 35, 69

Allen, Marcus, 25, 170, 184-
185, 207

Aloha Bowl, 177

Alworth, Lance, 28, 63
career summary, 104

Alzado, Lyle, 96

Ameche, Alan, 24, 61, 99, 169

American Football Conference
(AFC), 62, 63, 64, 68, 136,
139, 146, 151
team histories, 22-29
structure of, 20-21

American Football League (AFL),
19, 22-28, 50, 65, 66, 67,
68, 92, 96, 100, 104, 106,
163, 172, 206
championship games, 62-64

American Professional Football
Association, 11, 29, 87

American Professional Football
Conference, 11

Anaheim Stadium, 32

Andersen, Morten, 127

Anderson, Dick, 26

Anderson, Heartley, 219

Anderson, Ken, 22, 73, 161

Anderson, Ottis, 31, 82
career summary, 104

Anderson, Willie "Flipper," 161

Annapolis (United States Naval
Academy), 101

arena football, 84

Arizona Cardinals, 21
franchise record, 146
history of, 29

Arizona State University, 179

Arkansas, University of, 174,
178, 180, 182, 183

Arrowhead Stadium, 25

Associated Press, 172, 199

Atkins, Doug, 30, 246

Atkinson, George, 25

Atlanta Falcons, 21, 35, 91-92,
147, 151, 152
franchise record, 146
history of, 29

C

Cafego, George, 150

Calas, Pete, 87

Calgary Stampeders, 101, 155, 158, 160, 162, 165

California, University of, 151, 163, 194, 196-197, 203

California Bowl, 177, 246

Camerer, Dave, 199

Camp, Walter, 7-8

Campbell, Bob, 200

Campbell, Earl, 24, 151, 153, 169, 171-172, 185
career summary, 108

Canadian Football League (CFL), 101, 135, 154-165

Canadian Football League Hall of Fame, 162

Candlestick Park, 34

Cannon, Billy, 24, 63, 150, 169, 171, 172

Canton Bulldogs, 10, 11, 15, 17

Cappelletti, Gino, 26

Cappelletti, John, 169

Carlisle College, 17, 218

Carlisle Indian School, 9

Carmichael, Harold, 34

Carolina Panthers, 19, 36

Carpenter, Bill, 200

Carter, Michael, 96

Casey, Bernie, 34

Cassady, Howard "Hopalong," 31, 169

Central Michigan University, 187

chains, 224

Champi, Frank, 197-198

Chandler, Don, 67

Chandler, Wes, 28, 33

Chicago, University of, 17, 150, 168

Chicago Bears, 21, 27, 41, 46-47, 49, 53, 54, 70, 81, 84, 88, 90, 98, 99, 101, 106, 107, 118-119, 120, 128, 129, 133, 142, 145, 147, 149, 150, 207, 208, 210, 215, 218, 220, 246
championship games, 56, 57, 58, 60, 62
franchise record, 146
history of, 30
in Super Bowl, 76

Chicago Cardinals, 38-39, 85, 114, 142, 147, 150
championship games, 58
history of, 31

Chicago Stadium, 84

Chicago Staleys, 11

Chinese Bandits, 204

Christiansen, Todd, 25

Cincinnati Bengals, 21, 72, 96, 118, 143, 147, 210, 214, 219
franchise record, 146
history of, 22
in Super Bowl, 73

Cincinnati Reds, 218

City of Brotherly Love, 34

Civil War, 16

Clark, Dwight, 34, 212

Clark, Harry, 41

Clements, Tom, 160

E

Easley, Kenny, 28
Eastern Kentucky University, 221
Edmonton Eskimos, 155, 158, 162, 164
Edwards, LaVell, 175, 190
coaching record, 162
Eisenhower, Dwight D., 219
Elkins, Larry, 151
Eller, Carl, 27
Elliott, John, 27
Ellis, William Webb, 6
Elway, John, 152, 196, 199
career summary, 128-129
Emtman, Steve, 152
encroachment, 226
end zone, 226
England, 4, 5, 6
Erickson, Dennis, 175
Esiason, Boomer, 22
Etcheverry, Sam "the Rifle," 161, 162
Eton, England, 6
Eureka College, 217
Evansville Crimson Giants, 18, 147
Evashevski, Forest, 174
Everett, Jim, 164
Ewbank, Weeb, 144
extra point, 226

F

fair catch, 226
Faulk, Marshall, 185

Fears, Tom, 32, 42, 50, 59
"fearsome foursome," 113
Feathers, Beattie, 40-41
Fencik, Gary, 30
Fenimore, Bob, 150
Ferguson, Joe, 22
field goal, 227
field judge, 235
Fiesta Bowl, 177, 246
Fischer, Pat, 31
Fiscus, Lawson, 13
Flaherty, Ray, 88
Florida, University of, 143, 182-183
Florida Citrus Bowl, 176, 246
Florida State University, 177-178, 180-183, 217
all-time record, 187
Flutie, Doug, 101, 160-161, 164, 170, 221
flying wedge, 6
Football Writers Association of America, 172
Ford, Danny, 175
Ford, Gerald, 218
Ford, Mariet, 196-197
Foreman, Chuck, 32
"Four Horsemen," 201
Fouts, Dan, 28, 209
Foxboro Stadium, 26
Francis, Sam, 150
Frank, Clint, 168
Frankford Yellow Jackets, 18

N

Nagurski, Bronko, 30, 56, 84, 246

Namath, Joe, 27, 40, 67, 80, 89, 100
career summary, 118

Nance, Jim, 26

National Collegiate Athletic Association (NCAA), 167, 177, 184, 217

National Football Conference (NFC), 19, 20, 21, 68, 133, 146
team histories, 29-36

National Football Foundation Hall of Fame, 221

National Football League (NFL), 10, 11, 18, 42, 65, 66, 67, 68, 139, 147, 149, 151, 159, 160, 161, 162, 163, 164, 165, 168, 170, 172, 186, 189, 192, 201, 207, 220, 221, 222, 233, 238, 246, 248, 249, 250
championship games, 55-64
coaches records, 141-145
historical moments, 83-94
past superstars, 103-125
present superstars, 126-140
records, 37-54, 146
team histories, 19-36
trivia, 95-102

Nave, Doyle, 195

Nebraska, University of, 150, 152, 169, 170, 177, 178, 180, 181, 182
all-time record, 187
national champions, 174

Neely, Ralph, 30

Nesser, Al, 14

Nesser, Frank, 14

Nesser, Fred, 14

Nesser, John, 14

Nesser, Phil, 14

Nesser, Ted, 14

Nesser family, 13-15

neutral zone, 228

Nevers, Ernie, 31, 38-39

Newark Tornadoes, 18

New England Patriots, 21, 46, 105, 111, 128, 149, 151, 152
franchise record, 146
history of, 26
in Super Bowl, 76

New Mexico, University of, 200

New Orleans Saints, 21, 44, 45, 94, 127, 138, 144, 147, 152
franchise record, 146
history of, 33

Newsome, Ozzie, 23

New York Bulldogs, 147

New York Giants (baseball), 221

New York Giants (football), 21, 24, 41, 81, 88, 90, 93, 99, 104, 112, 116, 122, 123, 143, 144, 147, 149, 150, 151, 211, 213, 221, 250
championship games, 56, 57, 58, 60, 61, 62
franchise record, 146
history of, 33
in Super Bowl, 76, 78

New York Jets, 21, 24, 46, 80, 89, 90, 132, 147, 149
franchise record, 146
history of, 27
in Super Bowl, 67

Q

R

S

U